To Clair

Judith Russell

To Clair

A NOVEL OF SUSPENSE

JUDITH RUSSELL

CHEROKEE PUBLISHING COMPANY
Atlanta, Georgia
2003

Library of Congress Cataloging-in-Publication Data

Russell, Judith.
  To Clair / Judith Russell:
  p. cm.
  ISBN 0-87797-307-5(alk. paper)
  I. Title.

PS3618.U75T6 2003
813'.54--dc21   2003046297

This book is printed on acid-free paper which conforms to the American
National Standard Z39.48-1984 *Permanence of Paper for Printed Library
Materials*. Paper that conforms to this standard's requirements for pH,
alkaline reserve and freedom from groundwood is anticipated to last several hundred years without significant deterioration under normal
library use and storage conditions.

This book is a work of fiction. Names, characters, places, and incidents
either are products of the author's imagination or are used fictitiously.
Any resemblance to actual events or locales or persons, living or dead, is
entirely coincidental.

Manufactured in the United States of America

ISBN: 0-87797-307-5

06 05 04 03   10 9 8 7 6 5 4 3 2 1

Edited by Candi Lace
Designed by Kenneth W. Boyd
Cover designed by Debra Jackson and Judith Russell
Composition by Chirby Design, Atlanta, Georgia

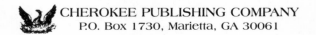
CHEROKEE PUBLISHING COMPANY
P.O. Box 1730, Marietta, GA 30061

Acknowledgments

THANK YOU

for the encouragement to write

— Bill Walsh

— Candi Lace

— Harriett Grisson

— Judith Winters

— Alexa Selph

— Ken Boyd

— and my mom,

for always encouraging me in

all my endeavors

ADDITIONAL ACKNOWLEDGMENTS

I would like to thank my two precious daughters, Laura
and Gail for being the wonderful people they are,
my chosen sisters, Mary and Jan, Ted Foret and his family
for putting up with me during this quest.

Thank you Debra, Starr, Suzette, Mona, Doreen, Jo Anne,
Harriett, Beverly, Sandra, Jane, Alice and Officer Mike for
the steadfast support over the years.

CHAPTER ONE

Fall 1991

CROUCHING BETWEEN TWO RAISED LEGS that Carla had carefully draped, Dr. Clair Weinstein adjusted her mask and turned the light on beside her. A sharp pain shot through her right temple. She had fully intended to stop by the lab for a couple of Motrin. Oh well, there was no time for her to think about that now. She pressed her gloved wrist hard against her temple for a second.

"Mrs. Campbell, I need for you to relax and move toward me just a little more."

The small woman, exposing her most private parts, was cold and frightened as she pushed herself toward the end of the table. "I'd like it if you would call me Linda," the patient said. "Everyone else does."

Clair straightened the paper under Linda as her

weight lifted from the examining table. "All right, Linda, that's fine, and most of my patients call me Dr. Clair. It's a lot shorter than Dr. Weinstein."

Linda smiled for a second allowing herself to relax just a little. "All right, Dr. Clair," she said, wishing she had not kept the appointment.

"Linda, I know this is easier said than done, but if you can relax, it won't be such an ordeal for you," Clair said. "Now I am going to examine you so take a few deep breaths through your mouth."

Clair noticed the small red lesions at the opening of the vagina and a moderate scratch on the peritoneum. "Okay, I see some minor cuts here," she mumbled while applying light pressure on the locations of the more inflamed areas. "Does this hurt?"

"Yes Dr. Weinstein!" Linda gasped and drew back. "I mean Dr. Clair, that does hurt. I've been usin' some cream that I got at the drugstore, but it still keeps stingin' when I go to the bathroom."

"I think I just found the source of your pain. It's no wonder you're having problems. Do you know how these scratches at the opening of your vagina might have happened?"

Linda was quiet for a few seconds. Either she was too embarrassed to talk about it, or a fabrication was in progress.

"These minor cuts down here are exposed to a lot of bacteria and it looks as if there is some inflammation, an indication of infection. Do you know how you got them?" she asked again.

"Well, Dr. Clair, the only thing I can think of, is that it might have happened after my husband and I had relations.   I might be causing it myself when I'm cleansing after." Linda was only partially lying. She raised her buttock off the table as Clair cautiously probed with her first two fingers to feel for tumors or anything else that shouldn't be there.

"Just relax and breathe through your mouth." Clair's voice was gentle and sympathetic.

Linda had never felt so ashamed in her life. "I'm okay," she said in a strained voice.

"I'm going to look inside now. Let me know if it's too uncomfortable. You have Carla to thank for this warm speculum. She tells me how miserable it is to feel an ice-cold instrument and I am the first to agree with her. I'd like you to take a few more deep breaths while I'm inserting it."

Linda smiled apprehensively pulling air into her lungs and slowly releasing it, as the foreign object was being pushed into her body. It hurt as she stared at the ceiling tiles trying to count the holes in each square. If she thought about the holes real hard, maybe it would help her stay still. She didn't want anyone looking at her like this, but she couldn't stand the stinging anymore either. It just kept getting worse. Dr. Sally Morris, the pharmacist at Compton's Drug Store whom she had reluctantly confided in, told her that Dr. Clair Weinstein was the best lady doctor around. With Center Ridge being so small, Linda was worried about her husband finding out. He would have one tantrum—no telling what he would do if he knew that she had her legs open like this for someone to see or touch her! Linda wouldn't and couldn't let that happen. She had taken money from her modest craft sales that she always kept hidden in the back of the pantry, in an old tin, to use for anything she didn't want Justin to know about.

"When was your last Pap?" Clair inquired reluctantly.

"My last what?"

"Pap smear."

"I'm sorry Dr. Clair, I'm not familiar with a Pap smear. I just want to get everything down there fixed so it don't hurt anymore."

"I understand, but a Pap is a simple test that lets us know if our female organs are healthy or not. It can alert me if there is cancer or anything else that could impair your health. If we know about these things in their early stages, treatment is far simpler and more effective. The whole procedure is very simple. I'd take a swab, like this, to get a specimen of the fluids in the lining of your vagina and send it off to the lab. After they do the test they will return the results to me and we will let you know."

"I'm sorry Dr. Clair, but I think I'd best wait to have that test, if that's all right?" As it was, she was taking a big chance on being seen. Adding one more way of being found out was just out of the question. This sounded way too risky. No, that Pap thing would probably never happen. Anything that would be sent to some strange lab that could be seen by just anybody was way too dangerous. The brotherhood had ways of finding these things out.

"That's fine, Linda, but I urge you to have one soon, especially if you have never had one. I advise my patients to have one each year. I am going to cauterize these cuts, and you will notice that you may have a dark discharge for a few days. This will help you heal a lot faster."

Linda wondered what being cauterized was, but did not want to ask. "Okay. Will it hurt?"

"No, it shouldn't hurt." Clair performed the procedure and removed the speculum.

"I'm going to examine your rectum, so do a little more deep breathing for me."

Linda had not expected this. "Ooooooh," escaped her lips as she felt a finger pushing into her bottom and moving all around. It felt really awful, sort of nasty! She groaned as the finger slid out of her. Linda felt embarrassment and shut her eyes and covered her face with her hands.

Clair stood and removed her gloves and mask. "I'm sorry for the discomfort, Linda. You can get dressed now and I'll talk to you in my office." Clair patted her on the arm and left.

Linda nodded with eyes still closed. Carla helped her get off the table and gave her a handful of soft paper towels.

Feeling messy and mortified, Linda used the towels to clean herself of the wet stuff Clair had used when she examined her.

A few minutes later, Linda sat on the edge of the sofa in Clair's office watching the woman with the short-cropped hair writing in a folder. Linda thought she looked very much like a schoolteacher, with those little glasses perched on her nose. There were so many framed diplomas on the walls behind Clair. She attempted to read them but was interrupted by the doctor's quiet voice.

"Well, Linda, everything appears normal at this point except for the inflammation I found on the scratches you have. Any break in the tissue can become infected easily because of all the bacteria that are in that area, as I told you during the exam. If we can locate the origin of those scratches, maybe you can keep this from happening again. For now, I am going to prescribe an antibiotic that will help you heal, and a cream that will make you feel a bit numb. I am also going to give you a light pain medication in case you need it. The cauterization will also speed up your healing. Now, I'd like to see you back here for a follow-up visit in ten days. Do you have any questions?"

Linda looked at her purse she was clutching tightly and urged, "Dr. Clair, I really don't want my husband to know. You see, I can't get a prescription at the drugstore because he would surely find out." She opened her small handbag and pulled out folded dollar bills. "I brought money to pay you today. I just can't let him know, and that's how it really is," she pleaded as her voice trailed into silence.

In cases like this, there was little point in arguing. "Well, all right Linda, I'll give you samples, and I strongly urge you to use this medication however you can."

When Linda left her office with her brown bag of samples, Clair felt a deep sadness. Whatever baggage this woman was carrying, the weight of it plummeted her like a steel cantilever.

"You don't send me flowers anymore," Neil Diamond sang to Clair as she drove through a shower of falling leaves, down the curves of Laurel Drive. She was tired. The twenty-minute drive home had only added to her fatigue, but at least her head was not throbbing anymore. She forgot to drop her car off at Bud's Auto Repair for service. Martin would gripe. She could already hear him. He always spoke his reproach as if she were not there. Women are totally inept when it comes to maintaining an automobile, he had said before. Well, what did it matter? Their relationship hadn't been what you could call passionate for a long time, and he certainly forfeited his right to judge—if he ever had the liberty to do so.

How long ago was it that the tall and sexy, redheaded night nurse had whetted Martin's adventurous appetite? That one had been the most painful because she was his first among the many who followed. Dr. Martin Weinstein had earned a reputation in anesthesiology. He was known for putting willing ladies on their backs without the need of Pentothal. The affairs passed the point of embarrassing Clair anymore. Martin was not handsome; he was tall and almost too thin but had a rugged, masculine quality that she, and most women, found extremely sensual. Piercing devilish eyes hid behind expensive rimmed glasses. A few sprigs of partially graying hair usually fell across his forehead. In the beginning their relationship had been fiery and exhilarating. Most of their friends had called it an ideal match. As physicians, they both understood the long, arduous hours. After Martin's affairs started, their intimacy slowly deteriorated by the continual deceptions and eventually, there wasn't a shred of it left. Martin had taken up residency in the large guestroom down the hall, an arrangement Clair felt more comfortable with.

Clair turned her car into the long, curving driveway and saw the freshly raked lawn. Old Henry Shier, a

German immigrant, had plant magic in his hands. The lawn was cleared of the old covering of leaves that had fallen making room for new ones that would soon take their place. Henry was almost fanatical about the landscape, and it was the one topic of conversation he relished in with fragments of broken English. She and Martin thoroughly appreciated the attention he had devoted to their home for fifteen years. They had oftentimes tried to become closer to the old man but he remained indifferent.

The Weinsteins had purchased the old seven-acre Donavan Estate nearly twenty years ago. They fell in love with it the first time the agent merrily drove them down the driveway. The stately, eighty-four-year-old, two-story English Tudor stood elegantly surrounded by perennial oaks and firs. The home was accompanied by colorful folklore of ghosts, murder and other strange occurrences that had supposedly taken place behind the old walls.

Stanford Donavan, an eccentric recluse, had surprised the community by wedding a beautiful young woman in hopes of carrying on the Donavan name. With all the attention that the raven-haired Marie Ann attracted from the eligible young men in Center Ridge, Donovan eventually confined her to the house with the exception of attending church on Sunday. He escorted her down the wooden aisle to the family pew at the Center Ridge Pentecostal Church, watching her every glance. After the service as he walked out, his hard black eyes would search the faces of the men for any eye contact with his wife. Their short marriage bore no children. One day into their second year of marriage the sheriff was called. It seems that Marie Ann had vanished. After a short investigation, it was determined that Marie Ann Donavan disappeared with a traveling theater company and was never seen again. However, no one ever heard of that particular group of thespians. The authorities never found any evidence of their existence anywhere, nor did a body ever show up. Some say old man Donavan had caught her with a young lover and killed them both. No one ever really knew what happened in the old house. The previous owners said they had seen a beautiful dark-haired lady roaming the halls upstairs and sometimes they even heard her sobbing in the night. This only added to the mystique and charm of the lovely old home. Now the residence contained the memories, the laughter and tears of the last nineteen years for her, Martin and their two teenage daughters. "Marie Ann" had yet to appear.

Clair was definitely not in the mood to argue with her daughter Paige. She had been nagging for days for permission to visit her friend Amanda's family lake house for the weekend for some sort of coed party. At this point, Clair had not been able to validate any legitimate adult chaperones. Clair had not relented. Paige used most of her usual tactics to get an okay short of a kicking and screaming tantrum. Young men and women with hormones racing like crazy were screaming for serious trouble if they spent the weekend together. This time Paige would have to take no for an answer and comply with house rules.

An evening chill careened with the approaching darkness. This time of year, when days become shorter, weariness comes sooner. She watched a large swarm of birds fly over and retreat beyond the trees that stood starkly in the graying sky.

Inside, the house was toasty. Clair felt hungry, but she needed to get rid of clinic odor. A glass of full-bodied wine and a warm bath always put everything in the right perspective.

She heard a door shut upstairs. Chris, her fifteen-year-old, would still be at cheerleading practice, so it had to be Paige. Clair bet that her daughter wouldn't try to deal with her until she was settled in and relaxed. She knew if Paige didn't get what she wanted from her, she would work on her father. Paige seemed to be annoyed by almost everything lately.

The cool glass of Ecco Domani felt good in her hand as she slowly walked up the stairway. On the landing she passed the collection of smiling faces looking at one another with love. A few were even mischievous. They were the faces of her family. The large museum-framed wedding portrait, she and Martin skiing, and pictures of the girls at different stages of development. Over the years, she had accepted this as a conditioning, a visual reminder that this family had shared happy times, which were rightfully enshrined in antique frames on the walls. Their two daughters had been the stabilizers that kept them together, and their lives had worked out with a moderate degree of tolerance.

Clair walked past Paige's closed door. "I'm home, honey," she announced, not expecting her to respond. And she didn't. For quite some time, Paige had been in her own self-serving world. It was probably a good thing that she would be going off to school in a couple of weeks. She had been a decent student, but a belligerent

attitude resulted in a lot of problems. Clair and Martin
both took a deep sigh of relief when they watched her
receive her diploma in front of the maroon velvet cur-
tains in the Center Ridge High Auditorium. For several
weeks now, they had been packing for her departure to
the University of Tennessee. Once each box was taped
up, an additional disagreement unfurled.

At the end of the hall Clair's room welcomed her.
Her room smelled of her perfumes, old wood, lavender
potpourri, and years of furniture polish and old dust
hiding in the crevices. The old wood floors were partially covered with vintage Oriental rugs. The eclectic
collection of furniture was friendly and understated, and
the walls were covered in old English wallpaper of an
intertwining pattern of ivy and light yellow tea roses.
This room had been her sanctuary just as Paige's room
was hers.

Ever since she had given up obstetrics, life had been
a lot saner for the Weinstein family. No more middle-of-
the-night deliveries. Delivering babies had become so
high risk in terms of malpractice it just wasn't worth it.
She could be at home more, and it gave her the luxury
of extra time with her girls without the burden of legal
hassles.

Clair scrutinized her body as she undressed. As the
mirror began to steam up, she could see the extended
hips and the disappearing waistline. "I suppose my
breasts are still okay," she observed, cupping each one in
her hands. "I wish I had more time to exercise.
Bernadette Peters, if I could have a body like yours, I'd
give up my Mercedes!" Clair wished she could blame
Martin's adultery on a midlife crisis but his indiscretions

had started long ago. Firm young women were the sweet rewards for men who thought with their lower brains—it was an agonizing fact. She and Martin were now both forty-nine.

The hot bath water had steamed the mirror totally and she became invisible. Clair stepped into the tub and let the almost too-warm water cover her. "God, that feels wonderful," she murmured as her body temperature adjusted to the waters. The wine felt cool in her mouth, turning warm as it went down. Over the years, Clair had worked hard to isolate herself from her practice when she was home; sometimes she had succeeded. The water and the wine were unraveling all the tensions of the day, allowing her to slide into that comfortable place where there was only relaxation. The connection to the outside world evaporated for a while. In the quiet of her bath Clair drifted into a soft sleep.

The cooling water awakened her. Clair felt stiff as she stood and stepped out onto the mat. Her nipples ached from the cold. As she dried herself, she noticed the illuminated numbers of her clock read 6:40. She had not heard from Chris. Martin hadn't come home or called, but that was not unusual. He was often late without calling. She had stopped checking on his whereabouts a long time ago. She reminded herself that Chris probably had stayed for the Friday football pep rally. Suddenly the phone rang and startled her.

"Mom, it's me." Chris's voice was out of breath and excited. "Paige and I are going to stay for the game. Please, please! We won't be late, promise, Mom."

"Well, I guess," Clair muttered in her trance-like state.

"Thanks, Mom." Chris hung up before her mother

could say goodbye.

Wrapped in her towel, Clair dropped the receiver
back into the cradle. She felt a paralyzing electric shock
dash up her arm, and she was suddenly very awake.
The hair on her arms stood up as she heard herself gasp
in the silence. When did Paige leave or had she even
been here? She now heard the unmistakable sound of a
door closing again. Was that Martin? She started to call
his name, but the only sound coming from her lips was
a whisper. Something inside told her to stay very quiet.
Martin always acknowledged his presence with a greeting when he came home at normal times. Clair knew
that. Could Marie Ann Donavan be making her first visit
to her? Hadn't she heard of stories where ghosts opened
and closed doors and broke dishes? She stared at her
fingers as they curled around the beige receiver. It felt
cold as she placed it against her ear. The piercing signal
told her that a phone was off the hook somewhere else
in the house; she slammed it down.

Clair's room was quiet now, except for the faint hum
of the air circulator. She waited, transfixed. When she
picked up the receiver the second time, the signal had
stopped. Hadn't she heard something? Clair saw the
receiver resting in its cradle and never felt her towel fall
from her. Her mind was racing and she was standing
nude, shivering. If she just walked out as if she were
going to the kitchen, it was only a short distance to the
garage, and then she could get outside.

"Stay calm. You've handled emergencies before.
You're not the type to panic. You're going to be all
right," she consoled herself in a whisper. The lock
clicked softly as Clair pushed the doorknob in as quietly

as possible. Couldn't all this be the product of an over-worked imagination? But Clair had no idea what was on the other side of her door. In a few minutes Martin would tell her that he just didn't want to bother her while she was in the sanctuary of her bath.

She heard the pounding of her own heart. The muscles in the back of her neck were tightening, so she cautiously lowered herself into the chair by the window. Clair wondered if anyone could see her. She vacillated deliriously. *I am tired, maybe blowing all this out of proportion. I feel like I'm high up on a trapeze swinging back and forth with only blackness underneath me. My gut tells me something is very wrong. I clearly heard the door shut twice. I am sure of it! Once when I came in the house, and then again when I hung up after Chris's call.* She looked around her room to see if there was anything she didn't recognize. Everything looked the way it always had. *I'm trapped in my own fucking room! I could sit here all night and try and rationalize this like an idiot, but would it really solve the problem?*

Once again, Clair put her hand on the receiver. She didn't want to lift it, but she did. The familiar dial tone was not there. The phone was still off the hook. Someone was in her home. She replaced the receiver as carefully as she had lifted it.

Still shaking, she slipped on a pair of jeans and a sweatshirt and tied her tennis shoes. Thoughts of her girls and Martin were racing in her head. The girls wouldn't be home until the game was over, and that was usually after 10:30. Martin could be coming home any-time. Clair stood straight and still until her breathing slowed. She turned her lights off and waited by the switch for her eyes to acclimate to the darkness. Familiar forms appeared; she was now able to see. Clair walked to the window and looked down. The tall cedar trees that flanked the driveway cast long abstract shadows that resembled a procession of misshapen bodies parading to the house. Her bladder ached. It was full and needed to be emptied. This was one dumb time to have to pee, she thought. Her presence was clearly known, so she might as well go. It was either going to be on the toilet or in her jeans. The toilet seat was cold, and she felt relief as her bladder emptied. Clair wished her peeing were not so loud. "This could be the last time I do this in this lifetime," she whispered nervously as she dried herself.

She walked back to the window to plan her escape. She looked out the window again and found the shadows from the trees were gone. The lights downstairs were out. The night had become very black. Clair was now freezing and her shoulders ached. The fear and helplessness were strange emotions for her. She used to feel that way as a child. Awaking from a nightmare, immobilized in that short time when reality was still the dream.

Clair was trying with all her strength to stay composed. The intruder could be anywhere. It was dark, but she had the advantage of knowing every inch of the house. There was a small servant's stairway between her room and Martin's. It hadn't been used in years. That thing was built for this very night, to provide her a way to escape. Thank God for old servants who used to schlep food up to invalids and ladies of the house who had the luxury of staying in bed to eat, she thought.

As she turned the handle on her door, she heard the click of the lock releasing. *It's time now, Clair.* She opened it just enough to squeeze through. Clair was standing in the dark hallway. Her eyes searched for something unfamiliar while she consciously monitored her breathing so not to give her presence away. With her back against the wall, she moved toward the stairway door, a few yards ahead. Her head bumped against a picture frame. It had not fallen. She was almost there and, so far, the hallway appeared empty. She stood still for a few seconds peering for any movements or strange shapes she did not recognize. She saw a glimmer of light coming from downstairs. Maybe it was headlights. Martin! No, it couldn't be headlights. The light was coming from the wrong direction. The light flickered; maybe it was a flashlight. Her stomach growled loudly enough for her to hear it. *Oh please, not now!* She felt for the door to the narrow stairway and carefully opened it, sliding into the darkness. Her hands reached for the walls. Clair thought she heard someone walking. She closed the door silently and smelled the musty old wood and some other familiar scent. She had smelled it before but couldn't remember where. Clair focused on maneuvering down the unused stairway. Some new sense of survival had replaced her fear. She carefully planned her escape. The narrow stairway would take her to a landing, down a few more steps to the landing off the kitchen or she could continue on down to the basement.

Things had been moved around down there since Justin Campbell had built Martin's workshop a year ago. All of Martin's tools and equipment were moved to the new woodworking space. No one had taken the time to do the necessary organizing down there and she was not familiar with the new arrangement. Justin had built all those storage shelves and intricately placed items in different areas. There were still a lot of things in boxes that the housekeeper had not put away. The basement was not a good option. When she reached the kitchen, it would be a short run past the refrigerator, to the door that would get her to the garage. From the driveway, she could run for the road before her intruder would know she was gone. The other option was to just stand very still in the darkness. She might remain safe, but what about the girls and Martin? She had to keep her children from being hurt.

Clair braced her hands against the wooden walls, and carefully stepped down the old stairs. "Please don't creak," she whispered. She stepped onto the first landing, then down a few more steps. Clair found the metal knob and slowly opened the door into the kitchen. More silhouettes. As she moved from total darkness into a lighter area, Clair recognized the familiar shapes of her kitchen. There was only one dark shape between the refrigerator and the door she could not identify. It seemed to move slightly. This meant that she couldn't run directly to that door and to the garage as she had planned. The alternative route was to crawl along the cabinets, behind the island then into the dining room and out the French doors. Clair's senses were as sharp as she could ever remember. Crawling on her hands and knees, she reached the dining room and hid under the table. At once, strong narrow beams of light slid from one side of the room to the other. This time they were coming from outside. They had to be headlights. She waited and did not hear a car door. Clair tasted the metallic zest of fear in her mouth. She felt something closing in on her. She smelled it. Like a statue, she remained still for what seemed like forever.

Clair knew it was time to move. Creeping out from under the table, she stood up. Her frame lagged in slow motion as if she were playing a part in an old black and white film. She didn't see anyone around her. Then there was an indistinguishable sound, which seemed to come from far away. Clair tried to locate it but couldn't. There was no longer an opportunity to turn back. The French doors opened and the cold night air hit her body with a welcoming force. Whatever it was, it was close now.

She bolted and ran as if she had been running for years. As she turned into the driveway she hit against a body full force. Clair opened her mouth but there was no sound. She just couldn't surrender.

"Clair! Clair! What in hell is going on?" She felt hands grip her shoulders. "What's the matter?" It was Martin.

His hands were supporting her now. "Martin, someone's in the house! Hurry! Use your car phone! Call the police!" They ran to Martin's car, which was parked by the entrance. He dialed 911.

Martin couldn't believe how strangely disoriented his wife looked. This was totally out of character for her. Even when Paige had disappeared for a night after an arduous quarrel, Clair had remained rational. Now her large hazel eyes displayed panic.

"Why did you park here?"

"I pulled in the driveway and realized the lights on

the entrance posts were out so I backed up a bit to check them. When I came back, wham, you ran into me. God, Clair, you're shaking like a leaf."

It was true; she was shivering uncontrollably, and she couldn't keep her teeth from chattering as she and Martin stood in the cool night air. He wrapped his jacket around her and held her closely beside him.

"Clair, try and calm down. It's all going to be all right. Look at me. You are safe now. Can you tell me what happened?"

"I don't know where to begin. I thought Paige was home. I took a bath. Chris called. No, I fell asleep first then Chris called. She said that she and Paige would be home after the football game. I heard someone in the house with me; then, whoever it was turned the power off. See, I thought Paige had slammed her door when I got home. I just assumed it was her."

It didn't take long for the patrol car to arrive. Two officers approached them.

"There is someone in my house!" Clair worked at controlling her speech. "I don't know where, but they cut off my power."

Martin helped her into his car.

With pistols drawn, the two uniformed officers treaded into the darkness of the house. Soon Clair and Martin watched lights coming on in all the rooms as they waited in the car. Neither Clair nor Martin spoke.

The officers emerged from the darkness with their pistols in their holsters.

"Ma'am, we didn't find any evidence of anyone in your home. The power was not turned off when we went in and by the looks of things, nothing seemed to be tampered with. We checked your house from top to bottom and didn't find any evidence of a forced entry. Would you both like to come in and check to see if there is anything missing?"

"That's a good idea, officer," Martin said. He put his car in gear and drove into the garage.

The officers escorted Clair and Martin through their home while they checked their valuables and the two safes. Nothing appeared to be missing.

"Maybe they weren't here to steal anything," Clair suggested.

"Who has access to your home?"

"Only our family, the cleaning lady, and the grounds keeper, all of whom have had that access for many years. Nothing like this has ever happened before," Martin said.

"We are going to need a little more to go on, like a description. Dr. Weinstein, ma'am, anything you can think of may help."

Clair looked at Martin foolishly. "Right now, I can't think of anything. Look, I only heard breathing and footsteps and doors shutting. He left a phone off the hook so I couldn't call out, and he turned the power off, damn it. I think he was in my kitchen. He was probably all over the house. I'm not imagining things. I've been terrified since seven o'clock this evening."

"Yes ma'am. Maybe you'd both feel better not staying here tonight. Sometimes the light of day resolves things."

Martin looked obligingly at Clair. "It's okay, Clair, don't get upset."

She nodded, wondering why they were so incompetent. Surely they had overlooked something that would validate the fact that someone had gotten into her home.

"Thank you, officers. We appreciate your help, but we had best just stay here and wait for our daughters to get home from the ball game." Martin's voice was gentle.

"All right, Dr. Weinstein. We'll have a patrol car drive by periodically throughout the night. If you see or hear anything unusual, all you have to do is dial 911 We'll be nearby."

Martin and Clair walked the officers to the door. "Thank you both very much." Martin bade them goodnight.

Still feeling that something was still not quite right, Clair walked back into the house with Martin, who expressed his concern once more.

"You know, Clair, you seem really stressed lately. This is not like you at all. Maybe it's time to lighten up some. How about a trip? It's been a very long time since you and I have been away together."

Clair was consumed by exhaustion from the ordeal. Her intruder had left a defiling presence that resonated. "Sure, Martin, you are probably right. I suppose I could use a break," Clair said half-heartedly and looked back at the small space between the door and the refrigerator. There was nothing there now. Maybe she had been seeing things, and maybe there had been a temporary power problem. The house could have just creaked naturally, and sometimes drafts could open and close doors. Marie Ann Donavan slipped into her thoughts. Could it be the one and only? Nonsense! At this point, Clair didn't know anything except that she was very tired and didn't want to sleep alone. She eventually fell asleep with Martin snoring lightly beside her.

CHAPTER TWO

Spring 1992

THE MILD SOUTHERN WINTER CAME WITHOUT record-breaking freezes or unexpected warm days. It had been just an ordinary parade of days without any unusual meteorological occurrences. The Weinstein family's Hanukkah had been as uneventful as the winter season. Spring had slipped in quietly after a moderately rainy March, nourishing a brilliant display of new color.

Clair's busy day was drawing to a close. Charts were piled on the large mahogany desk ready to be filed. The waiting room had been full most of the day. The dog-eared copies of *Life*, *Today's Health* and *People* were strewn in disarray. All three practicing gynecologists had endured their share of patients, but Fridays were usually chaotic full-house days. Rachel Levin and Dennis Ethridge, Clair's partners were dragging when they left the clinic. The evening would be a welcome break for the trio and their spouses to enjoy dinner together at Rachel and Lynn's. The monthly dinners had usually given them quiet social time together and what they did during the day was seldom mentioned. Rachel had been Clair's confidant and Clair hers for many years. Through Clair's emotionally painful times with Martin, Rachel was there for her with support and steadfast caring. Lynn, Rachel's lover, was completely understanding of the time Rachel had spent with Clair during the "unfaithful husband trials." These two women had been the balance factor that she needed. Rachel had an uncanny talent for putting dilemmas in perspective and dealing with the situation reasonably.

Clair leaned back in her chair and reflected. Courtney Meyers, a young physical education teacher, was relieved to learn that she would not have to undergo an anticipated surgery. For the last three months, she had suffered from an inflamed lining in her uterus. It was so troublesome that she had to take a short leave of absence from her job. The two of them fought the difficult virus with persistence until the swollen anterior surface finally recovered.

Linda Campbell had been in again. This woman was a story from the Dark Ages. For some reason, she did not want her husband to know that she was seeing a doctor. Distress was painfully visible on Linda's face. A while back, Clair had treated her for small minor cuts in and around her vagina that healed without complications. She was back again with a recurrence of the same thing. Her husband, Justin, had seemed like a normal kind of fellow when he built Martin's woodworking shop, but something just didn't fit. This time, her excuse had been an itch that she had scratched too vigorously, and accidentally caused the irritation. She had attempted to explain that she had not realized her nails were so rough. During this examination, Clair had done a Pap smear, culture and cauterized the lesions. The lab would send her the results and she would allow Linda to call her for them. Clair hoped the report would offer a clue about the mysterious cuts. She had a suspicion Linda's husband could probably come up with some of the answers—if she were ever allowed to speak to him—but Linda made it clear that she could not let him know she had visited a physician because of their religion. Maybe they were playing with unconventional sex toys. It wouldn't be the first time Clair had run across this scenario.

It was time to go home. Clair thought of the tulips and azaleas that would greet her. The lawn was now a palette of brilliant color.

Last January, she and Martin had taken that trip to Aspen after the holiday. Fresh snow, great skiing, and a bit of magic had made it a trip she would never forget. All the tensions she had carried to those snow-covered mountains had remained there. When she returned home, she found herself much more relaxed and content. Martin had been more like his old self. Prior to the trip, they had not really shared any intimacy for years. Clair had protectively assured herself on the flight home that she still was not going to trust him too much and she didn't.

She was alone now. In a few minutes she would exchange this antiseptic air for the pollen-laden air outside. The piped music had been turned off; only the sounds of traffic and the hum of the fluorescent lights remained. Clair sat in the quiet, recollecting the conversations with her patients, hoping she had not missed something pertinent. Turning her chair toward the window, she saw through the partially opened blinds that it was still daylight. The traffic looked heavy and impatient. Paige drifted into her thoughts causing an ache in her heart. Hopefully her daughter had left Knoxville in a timely fashion and was on the interstate heading for home. At best she wouldn't arrive until nine or ten. Could it be possible that Paige was missing them as much as they were missing her? Despite the fact that a separation was a necessary remedy, all three of them had missed Paige terribly. It was a bigger adjustment than she had ever dreamed. The University of Tennessee was only a few hours away, but far enough to give Paige the privacy that she desired. Clair looked forward to seeing her and envisioned a warm reunion.

Sarah Lyles, a full-figured happy woman, resembling a Dutch farmer's wife, had worked for and adored the Weinstein family for many years. She had watched the little girls grow into young womanhood, and tended to both of them like a valiant grandmother. Her full porcelain face was Rubenesque with large green eyes that moved quickly without missing a thing. She loved this old home that she tended to three times a week. Sarah witnessed the pain that Clair had gone through when she caught her husband in his office with that redheaded trollop when she attempted to surprise him with lunch. She remembered how dignified Clair handled the despicable matter. She had stayed quiet the entire time. She helped Clair pack his belongings and move them to the guestroom. That's all there had been to it, except for the grieving Clair sustained behind her closed bedroom door. Despite the fact that Martin was a scoundrel, and she was the one who sent his laundry with make-up and lipstick marks to the cleaners, Sarah still couldn't help liking him. He was just one of those men who customarily lured women.

Paige had been hard on both her mother and father as a result of this disturbance. She was beautiful and deceptively fragile-looking. Her strong will and feeble appearance caused a great deal of friction for her and to all who were closely associated with her. She was a sharp contrast to her younger easygoing sister, whom nothing seemed to bother. No, nothing seemed to bother Chris, "Miss Happy-Go-Lucky." She was a very athletic girl who rarely spent the time in front of her mirror that her older sister did. If Chris wasn't listening to that crazy "progressive rock" music, she was out God knows where playing some kind of sport. Her mother had recently put a stop to her playing her music so loud, and sternly demanded that she wear headphones. Sarah had also found evidence that Chris was smoking, and was in a quandary as to whether to report it to her mother or not. She had to think of a way of revealing it without outright telling on Chris.

Sarah's favorite room in the old home was the renovated kitchen. It was the brightest room of all. The white cabinetry with the glass and mesh panels made her happy just to be there. It had everything any woman could want or need, compared to her own dark old kitchen with appliances that were basic bones. It would soon be time to go home. Each evening before leaving, Sarah would instinctively place the mail on the counter in the kitchen and the newspaper on the table between the two leather chairs in the den. She closed the back door, got into her '87 maroon Monte Carlo, and drove into the Friday afternoon traffic that would escort her home listlessly.

As Clair walked through the front door, she smelled furniture polish. The heady aroma of coffee drifted from the kitchen. "Smells like home," she said as she walked into the kitchen. Sarah had decorated the kitchen with bouquets of fresh yellow jonquils and red and pink tulips, which created an overwhelming splash of bright colors against all the white.

Feeling the warmth of the coffee in her hand, Clair wondered if they were to be at Lynn and Rachel's at 8:00 as usual. The end of the day had been so hectic that she couldn't remember what time Rachel had said. Dennis and his wife, Shelly, would be there too. Rachel had had a ten-year relationship with Lynn Phaff, a CPA in the second complex down from theirs. It was obvious the two women worked hard at their relationship and seemed to have a rare understanding of how to achieve happiness independently and together. Clair always respected the courage of her friend's candor and spirit. Lynn had missed her calling in life by not pursuing a career as a standup comedian. She had the rare ability to take serious issues and turn them into laughter. The two women kept everyone laughing many an evening.

Dennis and Shelly had been married for enough years to have separated twice and reconciled both times while raising their three boys. Over the years of sharing the practice together, the three physicians and their families had become close friends.

Earlier, Clair had not been anxious to go out, preferring to stay home and wait for Paige to arrive. However, she was now very much looking forward to spending a relaxing evening with friends. She stepped through the kitchen and realized that the incident last fall had all but disappeared from her mind. It no longer seemed real. Admittedly, she had been under a lot of stress at that time and wondered why she had even given it a thought. If she believed in ghosts she could blame it on Marie Ann Donavan, the reputed ghost of the old estate.

Her mood was daring. She hummed an old Sinatra favorite, "That's why the lady is a tramp," while choosing a simple red silk dress. She carefully laid it on the bed along with her red bra and panties. "She feels that cool wind in her hair...."

Clair eased herself into the warm, perfumed water, thinking how ritualistic her bathing had become and how much she looked forward to it. The fragrance of the bath was sensuous. She closed her eyes and slowly rubbed her arms and breasts, then trailed around her navel lightly with her fingertips. As the soap slid across her wet skin, Clair allowed a fantasy to emerge and replace her outside world. She couldn't remember the last time she brought herself to climax.

The young man walked toward her, leaving the sparkling surf behind him. He was nude and golden from the late afternoon sun. As he sat on the towel beside her, his large blue eyes studied her body. She felt them as she also felt his gentle fingers lowering the straps of her bathing suit exposing only the slim line of her pink nipple. He traced it with his fingertip causing her to feel the pleasure deep down inside. She also felt the strong pulsing of her own erection. He gently laid her down, pulled her bathing suit off, and tossed it aside. Now his flesh was warm against her. His lips were impulsive and hungry, and he tasted of salt water. She wanted to taste and explore all of him. This young man was strong and hard, and she wanted to feel him straddle her completely. She felt him pushing his way into her until she was throbbing. Her body convulsed, and she gasped like a woman laid totally open to her passion. Clair felt the arms of comfort wrapping around her, and her body relaxed in the water.

She was not anxious to get out, and didn't; she just enjoyed the warmth around her and remembered what happened last January with Martin.

The stone fireplace made the room gold and warm that night at the condo in Aspen, and had ignited a fire in her. Martin had come to her that night for the first time in a long, long time. After a full day of skiing, a good dinner, and too much wine, he had suggested a foot massage in the warm glow of the fire. The massage had triggered a series of arousing memories and the passion that was suppressed between them for so long came in a raging flood. His large hands were strong, and his dark eyes saw the desire in her. They made love all night and in between they just held each other, sleeping only in intermittent stages. She had wanted to let herself go and love him as she had before. How long had it been since she had felt so fragile and vulnerable? Neither of them made any promises. She could not take down that wall that protected her.

With reality returning, she looked at her hands and saw that they were wrinkled. "I could go to sleep in a New York heartbeat, but I had best get my butt out of here. I have a dinner date to keep. Better get out now," she almost sang.

Clair was warm and content as she dried and wrapped the towel around herself. After drying she dropped the towel to the floor and reached for the red panties she had put on her bed. They were not there. Maybe they had fallen on the other side. After an inspection on the floor and under the bed and the dress, she still couldn't find them. Clair stood nude by her bed and felt the same sickening fear that she had felt once before. She quickly opened the drawer and rummaged through it. Nothing. Clair stood looking around her room. She clearly remembered putting her bra and panties on the bed.

"Who are you? What do you want?" she whispered. Her confusion was almost maddening. She felt someone there, very near. Just like before. Clair felt her chest tightening and had difficulty breathing.

Mechanically, she pulled her robe from its hook, put it on and ran downstairs. She hurried out the front door, down the driveway and all the way to the road without looking back.

"Help me!" she screamed at passing cars. "Someone please help me!" A few passed by as if they didn't see her. Two more cars slowed down, but neither one stopped. The next vehicle did stop. She recognized the

shiny black Ford pickup that belonged to Justin
Campbell. He stopped on the side of the road and
lowered the tinted electric window. "What's wrong, Dr.
Weinstein?"

"I need to call the police. There is someone in my
house!" She felt his eyes crawling down from her face to
the opening in her robe as she jumped up onto the
leather-like seat. It gave her an unsettling feeling as she
tightened her grip on her robe. What had happened to
this wonderful day? "Just get me to a phone, any phone.
The Mini-Mart."

Justin sped to the convenience store two blocks
away, where he parked his truck close beside the outside
telephone. He gave her a handful of change to call the
police. Afterwards, he drove her back home in silence.
They pulled up alongside Martin.

As he approached the truck and saw Clair disheveled
and frightened he helped her down. "What's wrong,
Clair?" Martin asked.

Tightly gripping the front of her robe together she
retorted, "Someone's in the house!" Clair did not recognize the shrill voice that was coming from her lips. She
felt resentment forming inside as Martin wearily put an
arm around her.

The patrol car stopped behind Martin's. He calmly
explained that his wife thought that there had been an
intrusion and asked them to search the house.

Clair glanced at Justin and briefly thought of his wife
Linda's visit to the clinic that morning.

"Dr. Weinstein, if you don't need me anymore I'll be
goin' home. My wife will start to worry. You know how
the womenfolk are." He winked at Martin.

"Justin, I really appreciate your help. I don't know what could have happened if you hadn't come along when you did." The two men shook hands and Justin got into his truck and hastened down the tree-lined road.

The police returned after a twenty-minute search. Once again, there was not a hint of any kind of forced entry. Clair felt sick and angry. She wondered what the hell was going on.

Martin was not concealing the aggravation he felt. "Let's get in the house, before you freeze to death." They walked into the house, both feeling their own individual frustrations. "I'll call Lynn and Rachel. We'll stay home this evening, and you can tell me every detail you can remember. Maybe we can put our brilliant minds together and attempt to make some sense of this. Clair, I'm here, and I really want to help you, but you've got to admit, there's no evidence of anyone being here."

"Martin, I am not crazy, maybe overworked, and tired sometimes, but I am not crazy or hallucinating," she said with conviction. "Damn it, I am an intelligent woman. I know someone was here with me in this house. I felt them with me." They walked up the stairs and only after entering her room did she start recalling how she had, without a doubt, placed her underwear and dress on the bed before bathing. "When I couldn't find the panties, that's when I felt the presence of someone else in the room with me. I couldn't see them but I knew they were there. Martin, haven't you ever felt someone breathing over your shoulder and turned around to find no one there?"

"Well I guess I have," he answered.

"Honestly I think I smelled something like an old after-shave," Clair recalled, feeling the hairs on her arms stand. "Yes, I did smell something very distinct."

"Are you hungry?" Martin asked indifferently. Clair shook her head and sat on the bed. Food was not an option for her swiveling stomach.

"I am just very weary and confused. This is the second time I've gone through something like this within a year. Martin, what are you thinking about all of this craziness?"

"Honestly at this moment, I am worried about your welfare and health. If the family is in jeopardy, I want to protect them. The idea that someone can come into our home without detection is frightening. We might need to update our security system. I am just as confused as you." He looked at her critically. "Why don't you take an Ambien? You will probably need help getting to sleep tonight."

"Not a bad idea!" She reached into her bottom nightstand drawer and found the bottle of white tablets. One fell into her palm and she shuffled into the bathroom for water to wash it down. When she returned to the bed, Martin began helping her into her pajamas. After he had tucked her in, he asked if she wanted the door shut.

"Hell no. I am going to leave my light on too. Thank you." She laid awake as long as the drug allowed, and drifted away without anymore fear.

Clair awoke to the sound of her daughters' voices as they were coming up the stairs.

"Hey Mom," Chris and Paige greeted her cheerfully.

"Are you both doing okay this morning?" Clair asked groggily.

"Dad told us he would remove our vocal cords if we woke you up. He said that you got very upset last night," Paige said attempting to lift her mother's spirits.

Clair reached up and hugged her. "I'm so glad to see you. I miss you so much. This house is just not the same without you. Do you know that?" she said looking into a young woman face who now carried a new look of independence. "What time did you get in last night?"

"I miss you too, Mom. I got to leave a lot earlier than I thought." She sat on the bed beside her mother. "So what's going on here? Are we having 'intruders' again?"

"I'm not sure. As it stands now, there was no evidence of any entry, and I am totally confused about the whole thing. It's so subtle. If anything is really happening here, it's almost impossible to detect. Then, there is the possibility that my imagination is working overtime. If that is the case, girls, my mind is playing tricks on me, and I'm getting old and forgetful. Who knows? I'm going to get some rest this weekend and see if that helps."

Paige waved a kiss and ran to answer the extension phone in her room. Clair's had been turned off to allow her to sleep.

"Mom, a 'Mr. Campbell' called earlier and wanted to know how you are feeling," Chris announced as she took her sister's place on the bed.

"What did you tell him?"

"Nothing, except that you were okay. Who is he?"

"Don't you remember the big man that built your father's workshop? Remember he used to bring his son with him once in a while?"

"Oh yeah, Justin, the man with the floating eye, and his weirdo son, Josh. I see Josh at school once in a while. He is really strange. Totally! They both gave me the creeps, and I really don't know why," Chris attested. Clair thought it interesting that her daughter had the same unnerving feelings about this man as she did.

"Why was he calling to check on you?"

"He *rescued* me last night. When I ran for help along the road in hysterics, like some sort of lunatic, he stopped and gave me a ride to the Mini-Mart so I could call the police," Clair responded tensely.

"That was nice of him ... I guess. Oh, Mrs. Lyles is bringing you a breakfast tray. She and Dad have decided that you should eat something."

"I don't think I could eat anything right now; although, dear daughter, I could really use a cup of coffee and a glass of juice. I'm dehydrated," she said, as she tasted the dryness in her mouth from the Ambien she had taken the night before.

Not realizing it was already 11:30, Clair ate all of her breakfast, surprisingly savoring every morsel. The eggs and toast had helped with the dull ache in her head. She briefly thought of calling Lynn to explain the dramatic episode. Martin had called them before she fell into a slumber, and she vaguely remembered him trying to explain what had happened. Clair laid back and pulled the covers up to allow her breakfast to settle. The warm sun was disappearing from her east window as noon approached. She relaxed into the darkness of sleep for the third time in less than twenty-four hours.

Puff pastries, cookies, and candy were stacked into pyramids of pastels. All the other guests were strangers. Yet, everyone seemed very friendly, as if they knew her. It was obviously a party. Everything was decorated with birthday paraphernalia, or was it some sort of anniversary celebration? A petite woman with large red lips and dark brown hair that was long enough to touch her buttocks, handed her a plate with cookies and candy. She smiled and turned away to talk to someone else. Clair graciously took it and tasted the candy; it was bitter as gall, and she spat it out. Everyone laughed wildly at her. The plate she was holding was knocked from her hands, and it shattered into tiny pieces of glass. All the people turned into shadows, and the outdoor garden party faded into dark woods. Limbs scratched her face and arms savagely as she ran. She looked down at her feet and hands; someone had tied silver ribbons around her wrists and ankles. They became so heavy that she couldn't run anymore.

Clair opened her eyes frantically to the familiar safety of her room. What a strange dream! She wondered how Freud would have interpreted this one. She found it fascinating to try to interpret her dreams. When she was younger she had kept dream journals. Clair promised herself that she would think more about this dream when her mind was clearer. After a short deliberation with herself, she decided not to get dressed. It was Saturday and she could stand a sufficient day off.

Her mind wandered once again to Justin Campbell and how he had leered at her. Clair wished she hadn't noticed what possibly could have been an erection when they were riding in his truck. Why had she looked? He had not overtly done anything offensive, but the leering was unmistakable.   The thought of exciting Justin Campbell was repulsive. In his truck, she noticed that his fingernails on his large callused hands were bitten to the quick. Had he tormented his wife with those daunting and jagged fingers? The thought of the two in bed together was inconceivable.

Toni Morrison's *Beloved* lay open across Clair's lap. Her concentration wasn't holding. She folded the corner of the page after failing to get involved in the lives of the old South and a culture that had lived in oppression. She got up and slipped on a pair of shorts and a T-shirt. The rest of the family was gone and enjoying their own Saturday activities. Clair walked through all the rooms of her home including the attic and basement. She checked the windows, making sure that they were locked securely. She looked for unusual marks on the windowsills and could not find any evidence of someone entering the house through these locked windows. Even so, Clair knew in the deepest part of herself that someone had been there.

CHAPTER THREE

SUNDAY MORNING WAS SUNNY AND LOOKED like it would stay that way all day. Martin suggested over breakfast that the family have a picnic at Castle Mountain. Neither Clair nor Martin was on call. The decision was unanimous.

Clair enjoyed the green countryside, and couldn't remember how long it had been since all four of them had piled into the car and headed off for an afternoon outing.

They all laughed and played and forgot about everything except the beautiful backdrop of flowers and warm sunshine. The predicted afternoon thundershower had graciously stayed at bay. The Kentucky Fried Chicken and usual trimmings were delicious and totally consumed. Everything was really all right.

Clair lay on her side on the large blanket under a big oak. Small beams of light shot through openings of the slowly moving leaves. She watched the ground and the lighted spots move ever so gracefully like dancers choreographed by the winds, then looked toward the lake and to the marvelous green meadow. Martin, Paige and Chris were tossing a bright orange disk that floated in the air from one to the other. They giggled and leaped, frequently missing it. Clair felt warm and safe inside. The fragrance of the grass and moss was incredible. Clair wondered when she had stopped fantasizing about making love in the woods with the erotic scent of old leaves and moss around her. As a young girl of about twelve, she had one of her first real introductions to sex under a large overturned root. It resembled a cave with wild vines thatched around the old underpinning. This was a private place to play at her grandmother's farm. She remembered asking her cousin Jeffrey and his friend Lisa, who were both thirteen, to go exploring for Indian arrowheads. Jeffrey pulled out a cigarette and lit it. Lisa and Clair both sat to wait for him to finish his cigarette. He sat on the ground, lowered his eyes and asked if they would let him look inside their panties for just a second or two.

"I just want to look for a second, I promise," he vowed. "All you have to do is pull your panties to the side a bit and let me look. You don't even have to pull your panties down. Honest, I just want to see what they really look like." In turn he would show his thing and the girls could see it grow.

Clair was repulsed. "No way!" she exclaimed. She knew if her parents ever found out, she would be confined to the house for a month. Why in the world would he want to see her anyway?

Lisa was sitting above him on one old vine-covered root. She moved her panties and shorts aside spontaneously, revealing the small folds that were lightly covered in dark hair. "You want to look at mine?" she inquired in a strange voice. Jeffrey's eyes were as large as they could physically be. He looked. No, he stared.

"Jeffrey! Stop staring, you goofus. This is not right. I'm going home," Clair said indignantly. "I mean it! This makes me sick as a dog!" She leaped up and almost ran back to the house. She had looked back one time to see Jeffery reaching up to touch Lisa.

Her reprimanded cousin looked so embarrassed Clair almost laughed, but it had only taken seconds for him to recover. Jeffrey had continued to paw at Lisa. Thank goodness she had not totally emasculated this young adventurous man who just wanted to look and maybe touch a little. Maybe she had secretly wanted to see Jeffrey's penis and show both of them her private parts. However, she had been way too shy about her beginning womanhood, and the strong values that her parents had given her were deeply instilled. That day in the old root, a new awareness had been born. Clair's thoughts came back to the present when her family wandered up the hill calling her to join them. She removed her hand from the folds of her shorts reluctantly.

Justin escorted his wife and two sons down the aisle to the second row on the right side of The Temple of Jesus Christ. Preacher Clower was sitting in his chair by the pulpit going through his notes and Holy Bible, already feeling the first dampening of perspiration. He took his neatly folded handkerchief from his pocket and dabbed his temples and upper lip. An assortment of churchgoers wandered in, and the rows of pews were quickly filled. The morning sun glowed furiously on the minimal clapboard building. A small wooden cross mounted the top. When the modest church had been built, there had not been enough money for a real steeple, so the builders just nailed a small handmade cross to the roof, under the insistence of Preacher Clower. There had to be a cross up there for the humble edifice to be a church. After that, no one remembered the steeple.

Preacher Clower stood up before his congregation, unbuttoned his light gray jacket, raised his right arm to the sky and looked at the pages of his Bible. "Praise Jesus. Glory! Glory! We come to you today to praise and glorify you, precious Lord." Preacher Clower lowered his arm, pointed to his book and shouted in a raspy scream, "But we are sinners!"

Preacher Clower lowered his Bible into a protective embrace. He paced back and forth on the small raised platform like he had seen Brother Jimmy do on his televised services. "You've got to give up your earthly desires and open your spirit up to him and glorify him only. Let him into you, like the light into darkness. Unless he is within you, there is no light, only the wretched darkness of sin. Ask yourselves this question, brothers and sisters. 'Who is the king of sin?' Oh, he has lots of names, but the most popular ones of today are Satan, Lucifer, Beelzebub, or maybe you like the devil better. He is always there. Always there when you least expect it, and he disguises himself in any costume he needs to lull you. He crawls into your house in the covers of the magazines you bring home from the grocery store. He sits on the ends of the tongues of some of the teachers who poison your children's minds." Affirmations praising Jesus accompanied Preacher Clower as he captured his congregation. "The music that comes into the car radio or headphones from some small tiny radio that can be carried around in your pocket is all about sin. The airwaves are full of slime they call music. Secret messages of the comin' of the anti-Christ are slippin' into your minds, young people. These songs celebrate the breaking of all of God's Commandments. The exploitation of cats mating with dogs and the world turning into a sewer of tattooed pierced mongrels runnin' in blind chaos, shooting mothers and fathers and each other, in the glory of Satan. Read the newspaper! Listen to the six o'clock news. Are we all blind to what is happenin' under our very noses?" Preacher Clower raised his Bible above his head in a pleading gesture. "Heavenly Father, what are we to do? How do we stop this tribulation?" He lowered his head and wiped the dripping sweat from his face with his wet handkerchief.

Justin's large work-stained hands rubbed excitedly back and forth on his muscular thighs. His eyes darted around the room in excitement. Justin felt the heat in his groin—that pulsing heat that hissed like a steaming kettle. He savored the feeling just above his testicles. Everyone was feeling the spirit on this morning, and church members felt it in the air like a heavy warm mist, right down to the marrow in their bones. Justin knew that soon the power would be his. He just waited for the Lord to call him and it was almost time; he was sure of that. Justin knew the Lord was directing him to nobility, every inch of the way. Soon, only seconds from now, he would be full of the Holy Spirit, so good, so pure. For a few sacred minutes he could be the vessel of God. Justin knew that this rapture was fleeting until someday, upon the calling, it would last forever.

He bolted to his feet and howled to heaven like a wild animal. There were no words, just a shrill howl. Then silence from the rocking, heaving congregation presided over The Temple of Jesus Christ. The only sound heard was Justin's heavy breathing. They all knew when one was called to speak in tongues. They always knew. Preacher Clower would know when Brother Campbell was called.

The large man dressed in his light blue shirt and dark brown slacks in the second row spoke in the unknown language to all the swaying arms that were raised up to God, to all the eyes that were caught in the holy experience. When Brother Campbell's prayers rang out for God to hear, they were in a language only he and God knew, resembling the sound of a record being played backwards. In the blinding light of heaven, that was the miracle and the special gift. Sister Doris Hayden and Brother Paul Talton related to the ancient language, for they were standing with their arms over their heads, swaying from side to side. As the others joined, the spell that only the Lord could grant paralyzed the congregation. "Praise Jesus! Praise Jesus!" every-one—even the children—screeched in unison.

While his father contorted in ecstasy, Josh Campbell sat still, staring straight ahead. He knew there was noth-ing in his life but the misery of his father's beatings. He saw the pain in his mother's eyes and heard her cries in the night during his father's preaching and praying. Josh stared because he felt contempt for the man standing beside him. Inside he wanted to run, to escape these crazy people. Why didn't Jesus help his mother? He looked at her and his younger brother. They, too, were standing and swaying back and forth, their eyes rolled back, reaching to "heaven" to please their Jesus. How pale his mother looked this morning. The light of the sun shone high now through the alternating aquamarine and white glass panes on the east side of the church. The smell of old wood and the musky odor of sweat and damp clothing permeated Josh's space. The faint scents of after-shave and perfume had completely disappeared. Josh wished the screaming and crying would stop. He wished he could go home, to his hiding place, and be safe from all the noise and the terrifying fits shaking the entire church. He didn't raise his hands, but he knew no one would notice. Not now.

The great storm within the walls of The Temple of Jesus Christ started to calm. Justin was coming back. His wet hair was clinging to his scalp. His whole body was soaked and reeked of sweat. As he returned to his earthly body, he felt chilled. "Praise Jesus, praise Jesus, thank you, Lord," was his last, almost inaudible mumbling. His temples throbbed and his mouth was dry. He opened his eyes and sat perfectly still. The anxiety would go away in a few minutes, but he reminded himself that Linda would have to be cleansed again.

Preacher Clower passed the collection plate. He thanked God for all his gifts. He begged for his forgiveness and protection against the devil. He promised the lowered faces before him "redemption and salvation," repeating the words multiple times. "Allow the Lord to save you," he concluded to the church procession.

The sun was now directly overhead. Church had run over, which was not unusual. The Campbells were fortunate to have their church close enough to walk to if the weather was not too hot or too cold, but this morning Justin had driven Linda's Ford wagon. A mile was never too far to walk for the Lord.

Linda put her apron on, determined to fry the chicken to Justin's satisfaction. She took the soaking chicken from the refrigerator and put it in the sink to wash again. As she rubbed the slippery pieces Linda looked out the window into the garden beyond the hedgerow. She thought of her own small and drafty home as a child. Her mama would pack newspapers around the windows to keep the winter winds from coming in. She and her brother Harold would huddle close to the wood stove to dress for school in the morning. All the while their mama would continue to stick the fire as she told them to hurry or they would be late. The sweet smell of the whole cakes that would come out of that oven had their mouths watering. Linda would never forget those wonderful smells that came out of her mama's kitchen when she prepared fresh foods from the root cellar, the mill or a neighbor's garden. Times sure had changed, considering most people preferred boxed meals from the grocery store or food shipped straight from some foreign country, Linda thought.

Living in rural farmland has been very lonely. Harold was her only playmate most of the time and the break from schoolwork was filled with chores that sometimes became play. Her mama and daddy were quiet folks.

Their words were few but stern, and she and Harold knew not to disobey because the strap would be waiting, along with "the Lord's wrath." Taught to be God-fearing Christians, they were taken to church each Sunday morning and on Wednesday evening for prayer service.

Linda started to fry the chicken. After stirring the peas, she set the table. This bright country kitchen was hers, and she loved it. It was the only room in the house that she had considerable authority over. The walnut-paneled den next to the kitchen was decorated with a deep comfortable colonial sofa and two matching recliners. A large print of Jesus, kneeling by a large stone, with the light of God shining down on his uplifted face, hung above the television. Across the room, a somber but compassionate portrait of him graced the sofa. On the paneling over the cabinets and counter that separated the den from the kitchen, hung small-framed scriptural writings in calligraphy. The remaining walls were decorated with stuffed small animals, along with fish and heads from past hunting quests. The drapes were usually drawn to keep light from glaring on the television screen. The richly carved gun cabinet that Justin had given himself for his thirty-eighth birthday was usually lit. The wrought iron and wood lamps cast eerie shadows and reflected light on the animals' glass eyes. The den should have felt warm and homey, but it didn't. Framed photographs of the boys and Justin's display of trophies from past hunting and fishing trips lined the hallway to the bedrooms.

Despite the dull pain between her legs, Linda busied herself in the kitchen with preparations for a grand Sunday dinner. Soon, the aroma of Justin's favorite meal filled his home. He opened the door to the meeting room and walked down the carpeted stairs. This large room was arranged with rows of folding chairs that had been collected through the years. Clean ashtrays were randomly scattered on the floor. A rectangular old Formica table was placed toward the back of the room. The brotherhood emblem accented by a large cross hung starkly on the back wall. Leaflets that pronounced the brotherhood's mission were neatly stacked on the table.

Justin spotted the small brass cross that he would need in a few hours. The cross had turned this table into his very own altar of sorts. When his brothers came to the meetings, they all had one objective—to carry out the works of the Lord. Sometimes it wasn't easy to please him, but most of the time it was downright pure joy. Once honored to be the chosen one, how could the consequences result in any emotion other than electrifying joy?

Josh and James sat on the front porch steps after changing into their jeans and T- shirts. James scratched in the dirt with a small twig.

"Josh, do you have a girlfriend?" James shyly asked.

Josh seemed a bit startled by his little brother's question. "Why are you askin' me? Have you found someone you like?"

"No, man, no, I don't have anyone really. I think this girl likes me. Well, I don't know, but I think she does. I really don't want to be bothered by no stinkin' girl, but I don't even know how to talk to her. See, Josh, she is always lookin' at me. Every time I look up she's lookin' at me. I don't know whether to smile or stick out my tongue. I just figured you've had some experience with this kind of thing," James stammered.

"Man, I try to not get within ten feet of a girl if I can help it. You are askin' the wrong dude. But what's her name?" Josh pried, nudging James on the shoulder playfully.

"Mandie Costello. She hasn't lived in Center Ridge for very long. Her dad works for General Electric and they were sent here by them." James sounded like a detective who just revealed a solid piece of evidence.

"Uh oh brother," Josh warned. "Daddy would have a fit! Isn't she that Italian girl that came last fall? If she is Italian, she's Catholic. If she's Catholic, according to Daddy, she is evil. How do you know so much about this chick anyway?" Josh drilled. "Sounds to me, James, like you have more than just a little interest here, which is not a good thing."

"I just wanted to know what to do if I do have to talk to this girl. Come on, Josh." James' inquisitive tone suddenly turned into a whine.

"James, you seem to be smitten. If you're wanting a little brotherly advice, you might not want to start anything with this girl," warned Josh. "If she don't go to our church, she's just out and that's it. Don't ask for the belt across your face more than you already get it."

The aroma of the fried chicken had drifted outside, and both boys suddenly found it a lot more interesting than Mandie Costello.

It was still early as Clair prepared for bed. Standing in her closet, her hands moved the hangers, idly to select an outfit for work. Monday mornings were always too busy to spend much time on wardrobe selection. Her skin tingled from being in the sun all day. What a glorious family day they all had. A small red item on the carpet under her blouses caught her eye. Clair leaned over and looked more closely. She pushed the blouses apart to reveal a crumpled pair of red panties. Clair started to pick them up but they looked strange. They were balled up in a stiff mound. "Martin!" she screamed. In a flash, Martin sprinted into her room with the girls trailing behind.

"Clair, where are you?" Martin yelled. He carefully stepped into the closet.

Clair's ashen face was staring at the small red object on the floor. She stood protectively hovering over her find.

"Call the police, now!" Clair spoke in a raspy command not taking her eyes from the floor.

Martin approached her. "Clair, what in the hell is it?"

"My missing red panties! They are covered with something, so don't touch them. I did not put them here. Do you understand?" she spoke slowly and deliberately to Martin and her daughters.

Martin dialed the police department. When he completed the call, he took Clair by the arm and guided her downstairs to the den. Paige and Chris followed, where they all sat and waited. She silently rehearsed what she would report to the police. Martin, Paige and Chris huddled on the couch together and fidgeted nervously.

When the police arrived, Clair and Martin directed them upstairs. One of the officers put on a pair of rubber gloves and his partner handed him a Ziploc bag.

"They do look a mite suspicious. Sure appears that they were used for somebody's pleasure catcher," he said quietly to his peer. Sergeant Ryan picked up the stiff wadded red lace panties, placed them in the plastic bag and sealed it.

"We'll run these through the lab and call you as soon as we get the results. If you don't hear from us by noon tomorrow, you might want to give us a call," the gloved officer said, not taking his eyes from the clear plastic bag. "Does anyone other than your family have access to your home?" He looked to Martin for a response.

Clair jumped in instead. "Yes, we have a lady that is here three days a week and an elderly man who keeps the grounds, but they wouldn't ever do anything to hurt this family. They've been with us for years and are above reproach."

"I will need to question them. It's routine, Dr. Weinstein. If you will kindly supply us with names, addresses and phone numbers it will save us a lot of time." The officer looked at his watch and wrote something on a notepad. "We're not accusing them of any crime," he assured her. As so many times before, the officer sympathized with these women in distress but he was never very expressive about it.

Later that evening a call came from the police station. "Dr. Weinstein, the lab report was pretty elementary and the results came in just a few minutes ago. I know you will be relieved to know that it was just odorless liquid soap splashed on your uh ... undergarment. Sure did make a lot of bubbles!" the officer snorted into the receiver.

Clair slammed the phone down in response to the jovial officer. She certainly was not relieved—not one damned bit. Her body was heavy and cold; even the sheets felt rigid and resistant. Everything was different now. The security of her room had been violated by a panty-thieving freak. "You fucking bastard," Clair whispered to no one. She knew that someone could get into her house, into her room, and get out without being detected. Clair promised herself she would scrutinize the entire yard for clues in the morning. She was thirsty, but too tired to refill the wineglass beside her bed. The anger and exhaustion were becoming more than she was able to carry any longer. She slipped into lethargy before the clangor of dishes and debate started downstairs.

Paige and Chris were finishing up in the kitchen.

"Do you suppose Mom is losing it?" Chris asked as she put up the last stack of plates.

The older sister answered arrogantly, "How would I know? I don't live here anymore. She should be better now, with me out of her hair."

"Come on, Paige, don't be shitty with me. You know, it is possible that Mom might have to be put in some hospital or a sanitarium," Chris retorted confidently.

The tall frame of their father stood in the doorway. "Don't worry, girls, your mom's going to be all right." He sounded strong and reassuring as he walked to his two daughters and embraced them. "We love your mother and we will all take good care of her. She's had some strange experiences that we just can't explain." His voice was not as convincing as he might have liked, but he felt sure the girls had not detected anything but unfeigned concern for their mother.

"She's down for the night, and I thought I might run to the hospital for a while," Martin said. He tried hard to stave off the urgency racking his nervous system. "I've got a staff meeting in the morning and I'm just not ready. Paper work will eat you alive if you don't stay on top of it. Page me if you need me."

"Sure, Dad. You go on. Chris and I will take care of Mom. I won't be going back to Knoxville until around noon tomorrow."

Martin was already over an hour late to take care of a very important matter at the hospital that didn't have anything to do with a conventional staff meeting. "If you guys don't mind, check on her before you go to bed, okay?"

Chris assured him she and Paige would forfeit going out that evening.

As Martin backed his Saab onto the street, he looked over his shoulder at the lighted kitchen and his daughters. He would know exactly where all three of them would be for the night. His attention turned fervently toward the road that would take him to his rendezvous.

Martin was tired. Julia, his latest, was becoming more and more demanding. She had become more of a task than a libidinous screw. Just what was her damn problem, anyway? Hadn't he sent her to that expensive spa in Boca and picked up the tab? What with the numerous gifts, he had certainly paid generously for his bedroom pleasures. Martin Weinstein had his own agenda, and once again, it was time to move on. After one more unctuous fuck, he would end this tiresome agreement. The practice he had in salvaging these hot alliances had become invaluable.

Clair came to his thoughts.   Her mental condition was slowly deteriorating.   Her patience had become short, and Martin wondered how much more it would take to send her into a total breakdown.   He could see the unease in her eyes that she tried to hide behind her smile and quiet demeanor.   He wondered if she was seeing someone else.

When Martin arrived at the hospital, he found Julia waiting in the staff lounge.   He could tell she was angry by her blank stare as he entered the tastelessly decorated room.

"Trouble at home.   Clair is sick. Well, she had a very bad day.   It is complicated," Martin stammered.   He knew mounting the fussy bitch was going to be more difficult than usual.

"Oh fine! I'm supposed to wait for an hour and a half while you pet on your wife because she had a bad day?" Julia spat out the words in haste.   "Please, you could come up with a better one than that! You're the one who invited me to have a rooftop quickie under the stars.

"Julia, I'm sorry about all this, but I am really too tired to argue.   I have had one hell of a day myself and if you want the truth, you are damn lucky I even made it here," Martin responded angrily.

"Well, why did you even bother to show up? I go on duty in ten minutes, and it takes longer than that to get you up." She stood abruptly, picking up her coat without so much as looking back and walked through the door.

Linda felt the pain in her lower abdomen. "Jesus, please forgive me," she wept silently, lying still in bed listening to her husband snore next to her. "Why are you punishing me for so long? Was it so great a sin, Lord? I didn't mean for it to happen. Jesus, I didn't even know what it was or that it was a sin." Something down there felt really different when Justin pried her legs apart and jabbed at her clitoris with the tip of his fat penis.

"I didn't know that I became of the flesh. I always hated it when Justin would get on top of me and do it. I always hated it, before that one night. I got so scared when it happened. Was it really Satan that caused it to feel so good that I lost control? Justin said it was. Did I really sin when I cried out that night? Justin said I did. Oh, precious Lord, if it was sinful in your eyes, I pray for your forgiveness. Please, dear Lord, forgive me." Her lips moved in the semi-darkness. "I am so sorry for my weakness. Jesus, I hurt so bad. I know you had lots worse pain when they hung you on that cross. I'm a poor example." Another sharp pain. This time she didn't suppress her outcry hard enough as she tightened her muscles.

Justin stirred and rolled over. The security light from outside revealed the wetness of her face.

"Pray, Linda. Pray harder. Cleanse your heart and spirit." His rank breath covered her face and made Her cringe.

She was irritated at herself for waking him. "I'm prayin' now, Justin."

"He'll forgive you if you confess and totally turn your life over to him, Linda." He rolled over as if God had spoken, and returned to snoring.

Her bladder was full and made the pain worse. As quietly as she could, she crept to the bathroom down the hall. She had a reason for not using their bathroom.

She wasn't going to make any unnecessary noise. After the pressure of the urine was gone, the stinging was unbearable. In the back of the cabinet behind the folded towels her hand found a small Kotex box. In her hiding place, she pulled out a white tube of antiseptic cream and a small sample pack of the pain pills Dr. Clair had given her. After carefully rubbing a small amount of the white cream on her swollen labia and swallowing two of the white pills, she put the remainder of them in the bottom of the box and pushed it as far back in the cabinet as it would go. She covered the package back up with the towels. The pain inside didn't go away completely, but it wasn't as bad. She slowly walked back to the bed she was beginning to hate with all her heart. Linda lay beside her husband, too tired to pray anymore.

After returning from his brief assignation with Julia, Martin could now relax and enjoy any new opportunities that might come his way. He knew she would page him the following day after her exasperation blew over. She had always been prone to tantrums but now was the time to ignore her page and hopefully close this weary relationship for good. "Heavy day!" Martin bellowed to himself in amusement. As he entered the house through the garage, he heard the television. He took a deep breath and walked down the hall, expecting to approach one of the girls still awake. Blue light cast its glow about the room, and a familiar hand hung limply over the arm of the large leather chair. Clasped in a childlike bundle was Clair asleep in front of the men on some sort of panel arguing about environmental issues. She looked so innocent and vulnerable. When he touched Clair's hand, her eyes shot open and she gasped in fear.

"It's me, honey," Martin said quietly.

"Whew, Martin, you scared the hell out of me!"

Martin held out his hand. "Come on. Let me help you up to your bed." Her hand reached up to him, and she let him help her to her feet. Clair wavered and he steadied her. Martin put his arm around his wife and walked her up the stairs to her room. He sat her down on the bed and lifted her legs, pulling the covers over her delicately like a protective father. Clair lay in bed, enjoying the endearment—even if it was simply dutiful or momentary. She wanted to feel the safety she used to, when the covers were pulled over her. She so clearly remembered as a little girl that the world was okay after the sheets and snug covers were pulled up high. She was shielded from all the bad things she could not see in the night.

"Martin?" she whispered.

Martin leaned close enough to detect the faint scent of wine and cinnamon. Clair's favorite combination of wine and graham crackers was unmistakable.

"Would you stay with me tonight?" Clair's request was rare.

After Martin undressed and slid against her, Clair sunk into the solace of his taut male form and fell quickly asleep. Martin wrapped his arm around her. She was completely still against him. Smelling the scent of her hair, he remembered how a long time ago Clair had been an assertive and responsive lover. Their love life had been adventurous and playful.

Then Janice had come along displaying short tight dresses that tenaciously cupped each ass cheek from underneath and pushed it up. That was just one of the lures that ensnared Martin. She also had those hard long legs that glistened and begged for physical contact. A man had to be made of steel to turn down what she laid out on a picnic table, so to speak. She was his first indiscretion at a time when he was not looking for anything outside of his marriage. Martin's reasoning was lucid: Janice had teased him for weeks, arousing him every time she brushed past him exhibiting small erect nipples in a uniform much too small for her bust. The bitch even looked dazzling in wrinkly green scrubs, he thought.

"Dr. Weinstein, the gall bladder is ready in number three," Janice cooed. All that red hair had been tucked inside her cap.

"Is that so, nurse?" Martin grazed his thigh lightly with the pen he was holding.

"Yes, doctor. Dr. Maynard is here. Looks like he is almost ready."

"So, I suppose it is time to put our patient to sleep," Martin spoke in a most intimate tone gawking at her mouth, wondering what she might taste like.

She just smiled and lowered her eyes. Martin had never been filled with so much lust, particularly in an operating room.

Martin remembered that after the gallbladder surgery as he had been absorbed in his post-operative paperwork in his cubicle-sized office, he saw—or rather smelled—Janice standing before him. She asked if he wanted some coffee.

The arousal flared immediately. It was uncomfortable as hell, which only added to his excitement.

Something down there was turned in the wrong direction and he realized that it was feeling painfully good. *Come on stupid, move the damn thing, before it breaks.* A broken dick was not to be taken lightly. However, any adjustment at this moment would be a dead giveaway, he concluded.

"You know, Miss Johnson, I think that would be a great idea. I'd love a cup." At this point, he would have gladly swallowed anything for the redheaded beauty.

"Black, right?" She knew exactly how he liked his coffee.

In the darkness, Clair stirred under his arm. He patted her stomach absent-mindedly. His thoughts were fastened on Janice.

When Janice disappeared from his small office, he shifted Rocky. That had been his dick's name for as long as he could remember. What fun he had discovered when he was about nine. That was about the time he had learned how to make Rocky happy. "Rockin' Rocky"—he was exactly that! Janice was giving them both a very good hard time.

It was late, and he had offered to walk Janice to her car, which was down in the bowels of the staff parking deck. As they approached the compact Volkswagen, Martin and Janice succinctly felt the rush of heat. She inserted her key and slowly turned the lock without taking her eyes from him. She ran her tongue over her sensuous lips making them slick and irresistible. Martin couldn't help his thick blazing erection any more than he could help breathing. He put his hand on top of hers, already consumed by images of fucking her inside the car. His mouth was on hers promptly as he opened the

car door. It was open and hungry. Janice's hand
clenched Rocky. Martin looked around to see that no
one was in sight, although he might not have cared if
they were. Martin was now void of any self-control.He
was absolutely going to blow it all with or without anything to sink it into. He laid her back onto the front seat
of the small car. His slacks were easily unzipped and
Rocky freed himself. Martin surveyed the parking deck
one more time.

As he leaned over Janice, he reached under her short
skirt to remove her panties only to discover that there
was no flimsy fabric to remove, just a very soft and
deliciously wet welcome.

It all happened so fast—too fast. The spontaneous
hunger and heat had been too much. Martin felt her
quiver and convulse under him, and that was all the
incentive he needed. He openly cursed at himself for
losing it so quickly. He had wanted to do so much more
to her, but the parking deck quickie was certainly nothing to complain about and there was less of a chance of
being caught.

"Dr. Weinstein, you sure pack a mean wallop!"
Janice's childlike squeal shifted the moment.

"Please call me Martin, dear lady. After all, we just
finished getting very acquainted."

As he raised up, Martin frowned at the wreckage. It
was surrounded by fur that was as red as her beautiful
mane tasseled around her flushed, radiant face.

"I'm sorry I've left you in such a mess."
Martin apologized.

Janice beamed a perfect smile and reached across
the seat, pulling a handful of Kleenex from a box. She

piled the stack between her legs and sat up. Even in that awkward moment, she was alluring.

Martin remembered the haze of guilt that taunted him on the way home. Clair was immersed in her career at the time and their life had become somewhat routine. Janice was so hot, but Martin vowed not to ever let this happen again. It was a vow that was not kept.

He fell asleep with a stirring erection and Clair snoozing close to him.

Josh lay staring at the ceiling over his bed. His father had threatened him again that evening about his grades. He didn't hate school, not really. Josh studied as hard as he could, considering some of the material Mr. Edmunds and Mrs. Crawford discussed in class was such a bore compared to the detective stories he loved so much. *Maybe I never will amount to anything and be a bum and servant of Satan.* Josh chuckled about his father's rants. He could still feel the marks of his father's fingers as he had gripped his arm to underscore the cruel insults he spat out. Josh glared at the tears on his mother's cheeks and the thin line of her mouth, too scared to speak. He wished he could go to sleep and find a little relief but it was impossible.

In the room across the hall, James' small body lay curled on his side thinking of whether Josh would take him to the lake and help him build a hut. He was worried that Josh wouldn't be allowed out of the house because of his studies. James sure loved building huts. He loved the sweet smell of the freshly snapped twigs. There were times when he and Josh had made them so good that even the rain couldn't get in. The bad part was that soon the fresh leaves wilted and died and they had to start over again. He and Josh would sometimes catch a fish and cook it on a fire. That was real camping.

James had never understood why Josh tried to make their daddy mad all the time, and the fighting terrified him enough to wet the bed occasionally. Oh, he had taken his share of licks from his daddy too, but Josh seemed to be getting it worse. James had noticed that his older brother's voice was changing and he was growing dark hairs on his face. Josh looked more like Mama and Uncle Harold than he did. Josh had a head full of unruly light brown hair and a few scattered freckles across his nose. In contrast, James' sandy blond straight hair, fair skin and light blue eyes created a softer presence. James had not moved a stitch in his bed. The security light outside revealed what looked like a million bugs flying around it, some big enough to be bats. He watched the fitful activity until his eyes could not stay open any longer.

CHAPTER FOUR

CLAIR WALKED THE HALL ON THE SECOND floor of Center Ridge General checking in on her patients. Her headache was banging in her temples as she laid the chart on the nurse's station and wrote more orders.

"Ms. Jones, have you got a couple of aspirins back there?" The request was beginning to serve as the question of the day.

After digging in the drawer of the counter, the young nurse handed her a bottle of aspirin. "Here you go, Doctor."

In spite of the pangs in her temple, Clair had good news. The rumors about her old classmate Dave Corn had been confirmed. He would be appointed to the staff of Center Ridge General in a few weeks. She was excited at the prospect of seeing him again on a regular basis. David Corn had been a brief lover and dependable, fun-loving friend from medical school. Clair couldn't help feeling twinges of premonition inside when she thought of his arrival. She wondered how much he might have physically aged after he had lost his wife and daughter. The small aircraft that was transporting them to a friend's wedding crashed in the North Georgia Mountains. After a year in solitude, he needed a location change. At the time, Clair had not been able to go to Maine for the funerals and although she had not seen him for three years, she was determined to make up for the lost time.

Clair turned to Ms. Jones once she gulped down the pills. "Call me stat if Lee Crayton shows anything abnormal. She could spike a temp, so keep a close eye on that catheter. I'm out of here. Hope you all have a non-eventful day." Clair got up from the computer and left.

The parking lot was almost full in front of the clinic of Etheridge, Weinstein, and Levin. They had occupied these offices for a little over twelve years.

"It's a full house out there, Dr. Weinstein. You are totally booked today and we are trying to work in some emergencies. Dr. Etheridge is at Center. Dr. Levin is seeing patients already and the rest of us are here. Thank God we aren't doing OB anymore!" Carla sighed dramatically.

Clair removed her jacket and put on her white lab coat, nodding.

"Here's your scheduled patient list." Carla handed her a sheet of paper as she taped one to the top of Clair's desk.

"Sorry I wasn't here earlier. Hope I'm not coming

down with something." Clair felt her temples throb from the headache that had become a nagging fixture in her body for several days.

Linda Campbell was her 1:30 appointment. Clair felt that same uneasiness that she felt when she had plopped down in Justin's truck the day of her "rescue." As her daughter reiterated that evening, the entire family was dysfunctional.

The morning kept Clair focused and busy. She didn't have a lot of time to realize that her headache had subsided. It was lunch and she gratefully sat at her desk and removed her shoes. She had taken two more aspirins, which finally diminished the pain.

"Carla, how was your lunch?"

"I'm dieting on yogurt and raw veggies for a while. My husband is going to start looking past me if I don't get some of this weight off," Carla affirmed with a pinch of her abdomen. "Diet shakes help, but they sure get old after a week or two."

"Carla, you are pretty, and the small amount of weight you've gained is certainly not unattractive on you," Clair remarked while silently wishing the 33-year-old's cliché statements about herself would eventually end. They had worked together for years and their conversations were always related to Carla's poor self-image.

"Thanks, Dr. Clair, but I'm not married to you." She laughed and handed Clair a chart. "Number two, Mrs. Campbell's ready. She is visibly upset, says she hurts a lot."

As Clair entered the examining room with Carla by her side, she gave her usual gentle greeting. "Good afternoon, Linda. What's going on?" She sat on the stool beside Linda and touched her pale, shaking arm. Clair sensed a pressing fever as she lowered her eyes to the chart. Linda's work-up showed 101 degrees, elevated white count and red cells in her urine.

"How bad is your pain, Linda?"

Linda's eyes were starting to fill. Tears ran down the sides of her face into her ears and hair as she tried to speak, but refrained.

"It's going to be okay. I am going to take a look and see what is going on down there, and just what we need to do to get you better," Clair said tenderly, handing her tissues from the counter along the wall.

"Dr. Clair, I just can't hardly stand it," Linda whispered. The tears propelled animalistic cries, then a sporadic attempt at composure. "My husband can't find out. He can't ever know I've come here. It's our religion, you know."

"I remember, Linda," Clair responded. Of course she remembered. Hadn't the shaken woman declared such for the last three visits? "Are you a Christian Scientist?" Clair was reluctant to mention that Justin had practically scooped her off their neighborhood street days before.

"No, we're Christian. We believe in our Savior Jesus Christ and the Bible. Justin is sometimes called by the Lord." She was beginning to calm down. "I just know this hurtin' is the Lord's punishment, I just know it is, Dr. Clair," she said in a softer voice, "I have sinned and he is punishing me. I must be cleansed of the devil. I know you don't understand all this, you bein' Jewish an' all."

Clair was now positioned on the stool between Linda's draped legs. She ignored Linda's comment, closely tending to the matter at hand. What was the woman doing to herself? The irritated labium was twice as swollen than she had seen the week before. She put on her gloves and mask. "Relax, Linda, I'm going to spray you with something that will make you feel a lot better. Now close your eyes and try breathing deeply. It will feel cold at first, but only for a few seconds. Tell me when you aren't hurting as much."

Linda felt the warmth of the light that Clair had turned on, the coolness of the spray that stung at first and the gentle touch of her hands as she made the pain around her vagina subside. Her breathing became congruous as she slightly flinched at the two needle stings.

"It don't hurt as much now," she said, experiencing comfort she had not felt for a while since the punishment began. The pressure of the metal speculum inside her provoked visions of her cleansing, as well as the birth of her two sons.

It had been the middle of winter in February when Josh decided to be born. He had come two weeks early, but Linda was so terribly excited. She had thought at the time of the birth that nothing in the world could have ever been more painful. Justin had been uncharacteristically thrilled too. He had called Sister Jenny Crenshaw, the midwife who always helped the wives of the men in the brotherhood, to assist in the delivery. Justin had joined the organization when they first got married. The members were all Christian and didn't trust the newborn to anyone

that wasn't one of their kind. She had both Josh and
James in the old dilapidated house that Justin's father
had given to them when they were married.   Then
Justin had built them the new house.   She had
thought it was the most beautiful house she had ever
seen in her life. And with pride, Justin carved a new
world for her in that kitchen because he knew that she
loved cooking so much. In fact, Linda didn't engage
in much else during the day besides taking care of the
home and preparing food.

She heard the music from the speaker above, and
watched Clair looking down at her.

The small, inflamed lesions she had been treating
in Linda's vagina and labia were not showing the healing they should have; there were also three fresh red
scratches. More infection was visible. The sight was
more disturbing than Clair could openly express in
the charts.

With ease and a sympathetic look, Carla handed
her a large syringe filled with the irrigating solution
she was going to use.

"This should help your infection and discomfort. I
can't tell you how important it is for you to take the
medicine I am going to give you. We've got to get this
cleared up soon. I will have to admit you to the hospital if this infection does not get considerably better very
soon," Clair instructed. She wished that she could do
more for this helpless woman than give medical orders
and prod her insides, but intimacy was not optional.
She saw the distress on Linda's face as she raised her
head up in alarm. Whatever the hell was going on in
her household, the fright was clearly unmitigated.

"I know we've been over this before, but I need to know the origin of these cuts so maybe I can help you keep them from reoccurring." Clair cauterized all the lesions and assured her that she would provide a stronger antibiotic. "I mean more samples, Linda. You don't have to get a prescription filled. Please relax," Clair said as she patted her hand. "Do you need more cream or pain pills?"

"I'm okay there. I still have some of both tucked in my uh... purse," Linda replied unsteadily. She wanted so bad to confide in someone, the isolation was almost unbearable at times. Clair instructed her to get dressed and return to her office to assess her condition.

Linda sat up and the numbness was still there. She was grateful. Linda thought that perhaps women should have been created numb from the beginning, not to ever have felt anything down there.

She dressed and Carla ushered her back to Clair's office, motioning for her to sit on the sofa in front of the big desk. She saw a picture of Clair, her husband and two girls. She knew that they were all Jewish, which she really didn't understand. Linda realized they had not been saved, and didn't even believe that Jesus was their savior. Weren't they the chosen people? How could they be so wicked and full of Satan? She remembered how Justin had talked so badly about them when he was building Dr. Weinstein's workshop.

"Is there anything you might like to talk about, Linda? You know, anything you say to me will be kept in the strictest of confidence." Clair was determined to extract something—anything—to use as a tool to help the woman, and she was damned sick of listening to the utter servility in her voice every time she mentioned her husband.

"No, I can't think of anything right now." Linda's smile was not convincing.

"Are you able to have intercourse?" Clair drilled.

"Not now," she lied. "Justin knows that I've been hurtin' pretty bad and he's been so good about not wantin' me to do anything if I'm not feelin' good. He prays for me and that the poison of the devil will leave soon. He is such a fine husband, Dr. Clair. The Lord speaks through him sometimes. How silly of me, I probably told you that already."

Clair nodded expressively and handed Linda three boxes of samples. She urged her to double up on applying the ointment after soaking in a soothing warm bath. Clair had no idea if Linda would make use of her suggestion but it didn't hurt to try.

Clair's two small sterile procedures in OR had been delayed for almost two hours. Everyone was rushing from ER to Radiology to OR. There had been a major multi-car accident on the interstate, which resulted in a number of atrocious injuries. Clair and her two patients waited for the availability of a small room. When she finally finished with her last patient, she washed up and wearily finished her rounds. Her body was telling her it was getting late and it was time to go home. She put on her coat and walked through the tunnel to the staff parking deck. The rows of florescent lights lit the enclosed rows of cars. Her designated slot was a little over halfway down just on the other side of the fourth concrete column. The only sound she heard was her own heels echoing through the deck. The security guard was new that evening; administration always changed them, it seemed. In the partial light, she turned the key into the slot, and saw a milky-looking substance running down the black door of her Mercedes Benz.

"What in the hell is this?" she queried to no one, looking around irritably and intent on discovering the person who had so carelessly soiled her car. She was mindful not to touch the substance as she got into the car. Now buckled behind the wheel, Clair drove from the garage.

Stopping on the way home, Clair picked up her dry cleaning and a bag of oranges and bananas from the grocery. She wondered about Linda. She had tried to question her both times about the origin of her mysterious injuries. "The Lord's punishment. Bullshit," she said aloud as she breezed through the front door. Clair walked up the stairs and into the shower room. She saw through the steamed door a beautiful masculine figure vigorously washing himself. Clair watched for a few minutes, cursing the adoration she still felt for Martin.

They greeted each other with a peck on the cheek as Martin strolled out of the bathroom in his favorite burgundy towel.

"How was your day?" Clair asked.

"Busy as hell. A real ball buster. Had a head-on collision this afternoon and they brought us six.

Two DOA's. We lost one during surgery and two are in ICU. The driver who caused the crash walked with a few bruises, or rather, was taken to jail," said Martin. "The son of a bitch was drunk. Two of the victims were kids." Martin nervously rubbed his right brow as he always did when he was extremely frustrated.

"I heard about the emergency when I made evening rounds but didn't get the details. I'm tired. I had a busy one too." Clair's words came out in a cantankerous rush. Her nagging headache emerged again. "I'm fixing coffee. Want some?" Linda Campbell, foreign spills on her car and now drunk drivers—the day was disastrous.

Martin gently declined, vowing to read something "mindless" and turn in early. Clair examined herself in the mirror. Her face was gaunt and very tired. The dark under her eyes looked unfriendly. She wondered if Martin's new interest was young. She wouldn't have black circles under her eyes or gray hair.

Her slippers were a grateful trade-off for the Nine West heels. She took two aspirins with water before pouring herself a cup of strong, aromatic coffee in the kitchen. The stack of mail waited on the end of the breakfast counter. One envelope was boldly marked "personal and confidential." It was hand-written and addressed to her. Clair opened it and unfolded a single sheet of notebook paper. The words were made up of letters cut from books and magazines and pasted neatly together.

Clair couldn't move. She only tasted the bile in her

TO Clair

You know you are Evil and less than VERmin

and You must BE Punished.

You will know our WraTH and VeNGeaNCe

YOU NEED to be CLean SED and purifiED

. YOU ARE a JEw BitCH WHOre

WHO TOUCHES WOMEN and contaminates them.

You Are GOING TO DiE.

The FOllOWER

mouth that usually precedes vomiting. Then she heard her voice. It was a strange singing sound underlining disbelief and confusion. "This can't be real! What kind of horrible joke is this?" Clair had never before received hate mail. Here was visual evidence that someone wanted her to die. She was not making all this up and her life was genuinely being threatened. She sank into a chair in the foyer and stared vacantly ahead. Not since her high school years had Clair experienced anti-Semitism, and then it was usually perpetrated by ignorant non-achievers. They always hated anyone that made them look inferior. Even then, she had understood the source was ignorance. When "Jew Bitch" had been written on her locker door, she was humiliated and disgusted, but she became aware over time just who had played this cruel trick. The offense didn't bother her anymore after that. The culprit had never threatened to kill her or even hurt her. It was just name-calling.

For a while Clair sat quietly. Her thoughts were abstract. She realized that whomever was responsible for the letter could have killed her in the tub or that first night in the kitchen. She reached for the phone and dialed the operator.

"Please connect me with the police department," she requested in the cold voice she did not recognize as her own.

As she waited for Sergeant Phillips from the Center Ridge Police Department to show up, Clair clutched the barbarous letter and stared at her surroundings. She was nauseous by the thought that someone had invaded her life so coercively.

Clair forgot about Martin upstairs. She sprang up

the stairs and found him propped up in bed reading. Martin was reading his latest edition of *Fine Woodworking.* She stood before him expressionless and handed him the note. He slowly read it and was on his feet. He seized her in his arms protectively, and she stood very still.

"Martin, I really don't understand this. I really don't. I've called the police and they're on the way over."

"I suppose I had better get dressed, honey. It's probably some Jesus freak. Clair, try to think. Is there a patient you can think of who might be involved in some extremist group?" Martin asked. He had never seen her look so empty. "What about the red-neck at the gas station?"

"Martin, I don't know. I need to think about all of this. Most of my patients are Christian. That's what Center Ridge is all about. Remember, we talked about that before we moved here. You know, we have never had the anti-Semitism that we had expected what, maybe nineteen years ago," Clair replied. "I haven't done any intentional harm to anyone. I hear about Jesus from many of my patients. I've got one now who is blaming her serrated vagina on the 'Lord's punishment.' I'm really too shocked to think straight. When the police get here I want them to look at my car, too. I think the soap bandit might have struck again. What an absolutely miserable fucking day." Clair rarely swore, but as she became more incensed, the profane language was almost a comfort.

"Hey, Mom, there's some man from the police department downstairs. What's going on?" Shocked by her mother's demeanor, Chris raced over to comfort her.

She looked at her father questionably.

"Chris, come on downstairs and listen to what we have to share with the police. Your mother has been threatened in a letter," Martin quietly explained to his daughter.

All three walked down the stairs together. Standing in the foyer was a tall, almost bald plain-clothed officer.

Sergeant John Phillips held out his hand with an open leather folder displaying a badge and ID. "I spoke with you earlier?" He looked at Clair and replaced the folder in his jacket pocket. He extended his hand to her and then to Martin.

"Martin Weinstein, Clair's husband. Come into the study and we will give you all the particulars. I am determined to figure out just what is going on around here, if, in fact, there is some sort of sick jokester out there terrorizing my wife. It's beginning to scare all of us." Martin sat down, directing Sergeant Phillips to sit in the leather chair beside him.

"Well, Dr. Weinstein, I brought the existing file. We've been out here three times and each time nothing was found except the panties that were loaded with dried soap." Phillips was clearly not as compassionate as he was on the phone. Or perhaps Clair imagined the trace of benevolence.

Martin handed the officer the note. "She received this letter this evening when she got home."

Phillips unfolded it and scanned the pasted-on letters and words that spelled out her death threat. The letters meticulously cut from various publications were straight out of some I-spy movie.

Chris sat quietly while the detective asked her

parents questions.

"Can you think of anyone who might have these feel-ings toward you? Maybe someone who is just a little strange?" Phillips asked. People usually dismissed the question; no one ever wanted to admit they had rivals—especially the wealthy and refined ones, as far as he was concerned. "I don't think there is any question that we are dealing with an anti-Semitic and obviously a very sexist one."

Clair was quick to respond that she was not acquainted with anyone crazy or hateful.

"How about patients? Is there anyone who might be angry about the results of a treatment or surgery?" With the severity of the threat, surely she could come up with something, he thought.

"There is no such thing as a one hundred percent success rate, but I've never been sued for anything or even received any serious complaints."

"Do you do abortions?" Phillips continued.

"No, I specialize in gynecology only. Sergeant Phillips, I've tried to figure out who can get into my house. I thought that after the panty incident, I was dealing with a voyeur. I just can't think of anyone." Her voice was becoming shaky and she cleared her throat attempting control.

"Can you think of anyone who might hate Jewish people?"

She thought for a minute, "Not really, although, most Christians think Jews are the persecutors of their savior. I honestly don't think that the people I know see me as Jewish. I think they know me as Dr. Clair. We don't even go to synagogue anymore. Somewhere through the years it sort of got lost in our busy schedules."

"How about you, Dr. Weinstien? Is there someone that you can think of who might dislike Jewish people or have a grudge against your wife?"

Martin felt uncomfortable. In his life there were several women who might hate Clair. He had been unkind, on several occasions, in the severing of a relationship. "Well, Sergeant, I'll have to think about this. At the moment, I can't think of anyone either. We've lived here a long time, and this is the first time we have had anything like this happen. In less than a year we have had obscure incidents, but this is the first physical sign that someone is after Clair."

Phillips wanted to speed this routine Q & A, and hit the nearest Burger King. He was so hungry, he could almost taste the golden hot fries and loaded Whopper. He insisted that the "cleaning lady and landscaper" would have to be questioned again.

"Sarah and Henry?"

"Don't worry," he said, shaking his pen at Clair. "We just want to know if they might have seen something else that would hint at some clues. I also have to talk to your daughter quickly if you don't mind." Phillips looked in Chris's direction.

Martin and Clair focused on their daughter, who had been silent until now.

"Sure, no prob. Ask away. I don't want anyone to hurt my mom." Chris was poised and folded her hands in her lap.

"Have you seen anyone outside this house or on the grounds, maybe just wandering around, that you did not recognize?" Phillips hoped the kid would be more helpful than her dumbfounded parents.

"Sometimes someone will wander up from the creek at the bottom of the hill out back, or maybe people looking for someone. Yeah, I've seen strangers that I did not recognize, but I don't remember anything unusual about it, and to be very honest I couldn't tell you the last time it happened."

"Can you think of anyone who might have a grudge against any member of this family? It is possible this person may be striking at your mother to hurt anyone of you or all of you."

"Sergeant, I don't know what's going on. This shit is all new to me," Chris giggled at the slip-up and apologized to Clair. Martin heard her swear all the time, but Clair was generally more strict about using such language. Phillips ignored the family dynamics, and pressed on with business. Although she seemed like a relatively innocent and charming kid, one never knew. He asked if she had any recent confrontations at school or more specifically, experienced anti-Semitism.

"Well, there are always weirdoes. Just a few skinheads with tattoos and religious freaks are there but I don't come in contact with them very often. Oh, I've heard mumbling about Jews and blacks, but until now there hasn't been any real serious trouble. Not many of the troublemakers take trig or upper level science classes. My friends are mostly Christian or nothing. There are very few Jewish kids my age. My sister and I are usually in the upper ten percent at school and we never paid a whole lot of attention to the background of our friends. It's just never been that important to us what ethnic background a person is."

"I want to know if any of you see anything out of place. I don't care how slight it may be. These are the things that could help us find some answers." Sergeant John Phillips wrote quietly for a few minutes and stood. "If that's all, I'll be going now."

Clair stood quickly, remembering the soap on her car that had been overshadowed by the letter. "No! I forgot. There is something else. Please come look at my car." She led everyone to the garage to the driver's side.

"This stuff here was on my car when I was leaving the hospital after my evening rounds. I didn't see anyone in our parking garage. It's not easy to get access to our underground staff parking deck. There is a security person and there is only one entrance, which is for hospital staff only," Clair informed the sergeant.

He asked for a spatula and a Ziploc bag. Phillips studied the dried milky solution that had run down the side of her car. Clair returned and handed him the generic tools for removing the foreign substance. He carefully scraped the remaining dried particles into the plastic bag and sealed it.

"Maybe it's the soap bandit again," Martin suggested, trying to lighten his wife's anxiety. He was surprised how skeletal and pale Clair's face appeared in the dim light. She faintly smiled. Fright was a difficult emotion to conceal, and she was through with playing the calm, resilient powerhouse—that he was sure of.

CHAPTER FIVE

ONDAY EVENINGS WERE USUALLY uneventful at the Campbell home except on meeting nights. Josh and James sat behind the garage in old fold-up lawn chairs. It was a place where they could sit far enough away from any prying eyes or ears. The spindly lagustrum bushes partially concealed them. They both liked watching the lightning bugs. Once in a while they caught a few and put them in jars until they were still and didn't blink light anymore.

"Daddy's meetin' is tonight. He told Mama. I heard him," James told Josh like it was a weighty secret. "She's in there bakin' while she's cookin' supper. It sure smells good."

"That'll keep him busy for tonight. He won't be preaching to us. He can preach to them brothers of his," Josh said through clenched teeth.

"Yeah, but Josh, I love Jesus! Don't you?" James dug his bare toes into the dirt making ten small holes that he quickly covered, then repeated the excavation.

"Don't know anymore," Josh replied as he looked out over the lawn to the freshly plowed garden. The doves were starting to coo. "Seems to me to be kinda crazy sometimes. I don't understand how Jesus can love you and sentence you to burn up if you don't hate some folks. James, it just don't make sense to me how people can be so unhappy lovin' Jesus."

"What do you mean, Josh? Like who?" James questioned his brother anxiously.

"Just look at Mama. Would you say she was full of joy from loving the Lord? Not."

"I don't want to burn up in hell for not believin', no sir, I sure don't. Josh, you gotta' believe. I don't want you to burn."

"Don't worry, James, I am going to take care of myself and Mama . . . and you too, and I am not goin' to burn anywhere," he said with conviction as he sat straight up in the rusty old chair, detecting something his brother could not.

James' big eyes stared at his older brother in fear. What was he thinking, talking like that? He silently asked the Lord to forgive his brother for he didn't understand his glory yet.

Josh's thoughts were different. He knew that the house would be noisy that evening. He couldn't hear what they were saying. There were just loud voices and the smell of cigarette smoke. Sometimes one of the men would forget his cigarettes or leave a long butt. Josh liked to have a smoke once in a while. His best friend,

Ronnie Seward usually had some and would share when they had an opportunity to sneak one.

"Boys!" Linda called them for an early dinner, which was usual for meeting nights. They both acknowledged her in unison and raced to the kitchen door.

After dinner, Josh and James marched to their rooms to do their assigned homework. They had strict instructions not to come out until they had completely finished. At least this time Justin didn't threaten them with beatings or other brutal consequences.

Justin sat at the long Formica table with six other brothers. He looked across the room at the faces that he had known for most of his life. There were only a few new men and they were good ones. They had proven that they could be trusted. Brother Charles Medders spoke of the proposed purchase of some properties by the government to build low-income housing nearby.

"Looks like we'll be getting about three new nigger-towns and it looks like Brother Johnson might be their close neighbor. Man, we just can't let this happen." The men stood, mutually commanding action.

"We need to get really worked up over this. Our community is at stake. Our children's safety is at stake here. I don't see any alternative but to stop it any way we can, and I think you all know what I'm talking about," Medders asserted. The faces in front of him looked eager to stifle anything that would put their families and their race in danger.

Justin felt his jaw clenching hard and his head was beginning to ache. He motioned and was recognized to speak. "Brothers, in the name of the Lord, we must protect our families. We don't want those niggers rapin' our wives and daughters—you know that's what will happen if hundreds of them are allowed to move in around us. Somehow we have got to put sanity back into the world. Clean it up and keep it from being trashed into a mongrel race. You know that this is happening everywhere. It's a plot by the government to destroy us. They don't want no pure race anymore. They are trying to destroy what God made. There is a war out there. The niggers are trying to rape and kill the whites, the Jews are trying to buy us out, and the Catholics are trying to get us to worship idols. The white race will survive because we will fight back. If we have to go in the darkness and take what is ours, then we will. Brother Leon in Atlanta sent us the report on the proposed purchase of parcels here in our county and it gives us a head start. We know what they want it for, so we can not let this purchase go through, no matter what."

Everyone cheered and Justin sat. It was time for the chatterbox Brother Gerald Crawford to chime in.

"Brothers we have another little matter that needs to be fixed if you know what I mean." Everyone gave him undivided attention. "Looks like to me that I seen this waitress, who is white, I might add, at the Steak House Restaurant last Thursday night behind the dumpster gettin' it from this big black buck. They was all over one another." Sounds of disgust came from the room. "I think y'all might agree it's time to do some house cleaning." Cheers filled the room.

The closing prayer was given and a deep sense of fellowship was cemented as they all held hands. It was time for refreshments.

The meeting was quite productive. Hearty solutions to the "nigger problem" were widely received. They gobbled up all the food and dazzled Linda with praise. And all the men bellowed and applauded obnoxiously when they jumped into their cars and pickups. Justin felt good, real good. He was satisfied they would resolve their problems, and he simply could not wait to tear into the leftover dessert. If there was anything he loved, it was chocolate meringue pie and chocolate chip cookies. Linda had made those cookies and Dooley Pruitt's wife had made the pies. Clarita Carter, L.D.'s wife had made a coconut cake, which he was not particularly fond of but pretended to be.

Justin climbed the stairs after dumping the paper plates and Styrofoam cups into the large trash can by the side of the storage room. The ashtrays could wait till morning. He hoped his wife would be asleep because he had some of his own homework to do before going to bed. He really loved the time he had all by himself so he could plan things without being interrupted. The upstairs was quiet and Linda had indeed gone to bed as he had hoped.

Justin unbuckled his belt and pants and sat in his chair in the dark den. He turned the lamp on and reached for his Bible. A passage from Matthew suited him just fine as he settled in.

> Woe to the world because of offenses! For offenses must come, but woe to that man by whom the offense comes! And if your hand or foot causes you to sin, cut it off and cast it

from you. It is better for you to enter into life
lame or maimed, rather than having two
hands or two feet, to be cast into the everlast-
ing fire. And if your eye causes you to sin,
pluck it out and cast it from you. It is better
for you to enter into life with one eye, rather
than two eyes, to be cast into hell fire.

The pages were soft and smooth. He had turned
them so many times and still loved the feel of the pages
just the same. There were many hours that his own
father made him sit with this very Bible in his hands. He
shuttered at the thought of the whippings he used to give
him as "retribution." If he got mad enough, he'd make
Justin sit in the shed out back, and more than once he
was left all night. It was to pray for forgiveness. In general, it was a hard time to grow up in. Times were bad
for farmers, but they had never been hungry. His mama
had always put a meal on the table, even if it was coon,
rabbit or squirrel. A few times family came to stay
because they didn't have any other place to go. The con-
sensus was that if it had not been for all the blacks and
Jews taking over, everything wouldn't have gotten so bad
for the Campbell family. He remembered his Uncle John
and Aunt Sueley telling him about the old Jew man at
the bank taking everything they owned. They had spent
all their lives working on that land before it was auctioned
off to the highest bidder. Justin knew this was Satan's
work. They were trying to get good Christian folks to go
out and commit crimes because they were hungry.
   "Lord, I know that Satan has slipped into my very
own home, in my very own blood son and wife. I know

that Satan is trying very hard to keep me from doing your work with the Jew woman. He works through that Jew bitch. He is usin' her to take me from you, Lord." Justin sat and chewed his fingernails and thought deeply about a suitable punishment. He shuffled the pages to Revelations and read from chapter nine.

> Then the fifth angel sounded: And I saw a star fallen from heaven to the earth. And to him was given the key to the bottomless pit. And he opened the bottomless pit, and smoke arose out of the pit like the smoke of a great furnace. And the sun and the air were darkened because of the smoke of the pit. Then out of the smoke locusts came upon the earth. And to them was given power, as the scorpions of the earth have power. They were commanded not to harm the grass of the earth, or any green thing, or any tree, but only those men who do not have the seal of God on their foreheads.

Justin looked up past the fan and textured ceiling, his eyes searching the shadows of the room. He wanted the sheet rock, wood and roofing to open to the heavens and send him his sign in a great white light and vision.

"I am waiting for the sign from you, dear Lord. I'm your obedient servant. I know that the purity of the white race must survive. I know it is our duty to preserve all that is sanctified, good and pure."

He closed his Bible and heard the sound of faraway thunder.

"Lord, I hope you will keep it clear tomorrow. I've got that addition for Jake Harrison to finish. Remember Lord, I've just plowed that garden out there."

Justin sat for a while, just thinking. He thought about Josh again, who was not being a good Christian boy at all. It was about time to take some hide and set him back a notch or two. Justin was certain the devil was trying to get a foothold on that child. He would force him to read his Bible more. "Spare the rod and spoil the child," his father would say. In honor of him, Justin would make both boys obey. James was no exception. A few red whelps never hurt anybody. In his eyes, he was the head of the house and had taken good care of all of them over the years. In deep thought Justin gnawed on his nails, which had been a habit ever since he could remember. When no one was around and he had quiet time, he could chew without anyone yelling or hitting his hands. His father used to lash out at him for chewing "on himself."

"Nasty, boy . . . pure nasty!" he would shout in front of anyone.

Justin just couldn't stop. His mama used to slap him in the face with his fingers still in his mouth. Once or twice he thought she had knocked out his teeth. His daddy didn't try to catch him. He would just look at his nails, and beat him if they appeared to be chewed. This meant that he got lots of whippings. Well, nobody could hit him now. Justin didn't feel comfortable chewing in front of folks. He did it when he was alone. The habit had gotten so bad his fingertips were coated with dried blood. If Linda ever noticed, she didn't say so.

Justin looked at one of the deer heads and remembered that Preacher Clower still had his deer stand. His eyes were getting heavy and he lovingly put his Bible back on the table. He zipped up his pants and walked down the dark hall to the bedroom.

By morning it was pouring rain, one of those heavy spring downpours that looked like it wouldn't ever quit. Putting a roof on any house was definitely not on the agenda. He would find other things to do though, real important things. First he had to get those boys moving because it was a school day.

CHAPTER SIX

THE WIPERS ON CLAIR'S CAR BOLTED LEFT to right frantically, and it was still difficult to see through the torrential rain. She was becoming anxious as she struggled to see through the waterfall on her windshield. It was dark and the roads were flooded. Clair needed to be scrubbed by seven. Headlights appeared out of nowhere so unexpectedly that she swerved, running over the curb. She straightened the car back onto the flooded surface that she only guessed to be safe. Clair was shaking so badly that she clamped her fingers hard on the steering wheel. The drive was only a little further before she reached the safety of the hospital. Finally, the cover of the lighted parking deck welcomed her, and the wipers banged back and forth without the interference of the rain.

The OR was brightly lit, busy and running full speed. The moving figures, dressed in green, were fresh and focused on getting everything ready. Clair had a tubal ligation to perform.

"Good morning, Dr. Weinstein."

"Morning, Donald." Her time was so limited, Clair had forgotten to look back and admire the surgical technician's physique.

As she rushed through to the lounge to pee and change, she was greeted by several of her peers. Clair dressed for surgery and briefly wondered about the lab results from the scrapings on her car.

"Clair, you're looking good this morning. Is Paige still loving the Big Orange?"

"Still does so far but I don't know if I do," she responded to her friend Tim Castle. He was an OB man at Center Ridge and really preferred delivering babies. Last year it had been rumored that Tim's wife and Martin had a "thing" but nothing much was said about it, so it became one of those matters that disappeared in time. Martin did have a reputation to maintain.

The morning procedure went without complication. Clair was able to have a quick cup of coffee with Martin before heading upstairs to make rounds. She put on her raincoat and walked briskly to her car. She noticed that the parking deck always smelled like a cave when it rained. The weather outside had subsided to a light downpour and the roads still carried the evidence of the earlier monsoons. She cautiously drove through the partially flooded streets.

Her headache returned. Maybe too much coffee, or not enough regular meals. When she arrived at the clinic, Clair took two aspirin and a few minutes to greet her partners and freshen up. She had been happy with the low maintenance of her new perm, but the rain had turned her hair into tiny unmanageable ringlets. A little lipstick and her lab coat were all she needed to meet her medical world. Clair reminded herself how much she loved what she did as she quickly applied her light rose lipstick.

In the darkness of the Weinsteins' basement that morning, wet shoes tracked through the scattered boxes. A large figure was making a delivery and hiding things in secret places while checking to see if anyone had tampered with the gear that was hidden before. Nobody was going to find anything down there because he had done a real good job of hiding everything just right. He was sure that even the police wouldn't look inside all the boxes. Upstairs the vacuum was being pushed back and forth. No one heard the noises in the basement.

Afternoon came fast. Martin got home before Clair. His day had been light and short and to his delight, he was not on call that evening. Martin was free as a bird, and for a change, he wasn't completely drained.

The den was warm and muggy. Rainy days always gave their old home a musty sort of smell, seemingly holding some of the moisture inside. He checked the mail, poured himself a cup of stale coffee and sat at the counter to read the evening paper.

Chris bounded through the kitchen door. "Dad, you're home!" She looked surprised as she dropped her books on the table and headed straight for the refrigerator.

"Yes, I had an easy day for a change," he answered as

he continued reading.

Chris took out the jelly and reached into the pantry for the peanut butter and bread.

"Want one, Dad?"

"No thanks, honey. I'm looking forward to dinner. There's lasagna in the fridge. I think that's what we're having. Aren't you going to spoil your dinner?" he asked, examining the very generous sandwich.

"Nope," she retorted and took a big bite, then returned to the fridge for a glass of milk.

This girl had a ravenous appetite and never gained an ounce. Clair was just like that before the birth of Paige. Chris had always been packed full of energy. She played softball and tennis, and had recently fallen in love with volleyball. Martin was very proud of both daughters. He folded the papers and sat back. "How's school?"

"Crazy right now. Prom's coming up. Term papers and everything else we have to do this time of year. I just might voluntarily go crazy. Seriously, Dad, I'm really ready for summer to get here." She looked at the clock on the wall. "I've got to call Mickey. We're supposed to go to the mall. She has her own car, Dad."

"She does, huh? I suppose it helps to be old enough to have a driver's license." He knew full well about Mickey's car. Chris was not going to let him forget for one minute that she had a birthday coming up and that she wanted a new car.

"Yes, Dad. She got it for her sixteenth birthday. It was a real surprise. She got up in the morning to have breakfast, and sitting beside her cereal spoon was a key. Wasn't that great?"

He intended to get her a car. He had already picked out a red Honda Prelude SI. He and Clair would surprise her at her party, and Paige was going to help. Paige had also gotten her vehicle when she was sixteen. It would just make life easier.

Martin heard the sound of Clair's car as it came down the driveway. When she walked into the kitchen, he sensed the tension.

"How was it, Clair?"

She shrugged and opened the fridge, putting the aluminum container into the oven. Clair removed her jacket and sat down.

"I hate to say this, but you look depleted of nutrients, rest and everything else," Martin said candidly. He tried to lighten his tone but the attempt was obscured by the reactive frown on her face. "How about a cup of this stale coffee?"

"Aspirin first, please. I've had this damn headache too long now. Sure wish I could get rid of it for more than a day," she said through almost unmoving lips as she massaged her temples and closed her eyes.

"Oh, guess what!"

Clair responded dully with her eyes still closed.

"You'll be relieved to know that the police called. It's not soap this time."

She piped up and opened her eyes. "Really? What in the world is it then?"

"Looks like someone slopped buttermilk on your door. Doesn't Cam Donaldson still park next to you?" Martin probed.

A smiling face answered, "Yes. When did they call?"

"Not until you had already left the hospital, then I

got busy and I guess it slipped my mind."

"What a relief! Can you believe it was buttermilk?"

"Ask him tomorrow if he had any passengers that drink buttermilk. At least this one doesn't seem to bother me so much," Martin remarked. "It was probably just an accident. With everything else going on around here, I suppose we all are a little edgy."

"I think you're right. It sure would be a simple solution if Cam did have a clumsy passenger. I'll ask tomorrow morning, sure thing."

Martin took the bottle of small white tablets from the shelf by the window and pushed a glass against the water dispenser on the refrigerator door. He handed both to Clair. "Why don't you see Carl Rufkin tomorrow? Maybe he could at least tell you if there is anything that needs to be examined promptly. You know, Clair, when you put this shit off . . ."

"I really don't need this from you," Clair interrupted him with a speedy reply. "It's a stupid tension or sinus headache. Besides, I've already planned to see Carl tomorrow, but thanks for the reminder," she said, wanting only silence. Her weariness had returned. She swallowed the aspirin, pushed each shoe off and sagged in the kitchen chair.

Relaxation was not coming easily. Clair stood abruptly, washed her hands and started to prepare the dinner salad.

Chris barreled into the kitchen, kissed her mother on the cheek and announced that she was off for some "serious window shopping" at the mall.

"Hi darling, I want you to eat first," Clair ordered.

"I'm not hungry, Mom, really I'm not," Chris grumbled and immediately picked up on the motherly neediness coming on.

"I don't get the opportunity to have all three of us eat dinner together very often. It would really be a treat for me. Please, eat with your father and I."

"Mom, Mickey will be here in a few minutes," Chris argued.

"It should be cooked by then. All I have to do is just heat it. Just invite her in for dinner." Clair's spirits were picking up at the thought of having a real family dinner. Chris would inevitably oblige her.

When Mickey came through the door, Chris pulled her by the arm. "Mom wants us to have dinner before we go so you are going to eat if I have to." Everyone heard Chris's murmured command. Clair and Martin smirked at each other.

"Hey, that's cool. We can just eat a little," Mickey said as she was ushered into the kitchen.

Chris had been scoping out prom dresses at Dillard's and wanted to try on a few. Actually, she also wanted enough time to hang out at the mall—Kenny would be waiting for her to get there. Nonetheless, she and Mickey ate an ample helping of hot lasagna. Clair relished in the brief meal. She had always loved the sound of girls chatting and giggling over the dinner table.

After dinner, when no one else was around, Clair looked out her bedroom window at the approaching evening and the familiar shadows that forged her view for so many years. She thought of the night last fall when they had dissolved and she sensed that someone was in her home. She had not taken the time to look around outside. The police had, but for some reason, Clair had not. She couldn't remember the last time Martin used his workshop or if he had even bothered looking around the property for anything out of the ordinary.

The Bible lay open across Justin's thighs and a finger lovingly caressed the words. It was almost like touching his Savior. The paper had a sensuous feel, sort of like silk, but better. It made a quiet sound, almost like whispers when he turned the pages. This book would guide him and advise him and comfort him. Justin felt the power from this book, as he prayed for purity and perfection in his life. Only a mortal sinner could be saved by letting the Lord Jesus Christ totally direct his life. Justin was still waiting for his voice or sign. He knew he would receive it soon. He just knew that as sure as he knew he was breathing. Justin turned to one of Preacher Clower's favorite readings from Thessalonians enthusiastically.

> Finally then, brethren, we urge and exhort in the Lord Jesus that you should abound more and more, just as you received from us how you ought to walk and to please God; for you know what commandments we gave you through the Lord Jesus. For this is the will of God, your sanctification: that you should abstain from sexual immorality; that each of you should know how to possess his own vessel in sanctification and honor, not in passion of lust, like the Gentiles who do not know God;

that no one should take advantage of or
defraud his brother in this matter, because the
Lord is the avenger of all such, as we also fore-
warned you and testified.

Justin felt the passion and washed himself with these
words from his precious book. These words were the
guiding force of his very existence.

The last bell rang at Center Ridge High, and Chris
and Mickey raced for the shiny red Rabbit. Mickey
stuck the key into the ignition and the engine started its
familiar putter. Chris and Mickey loved just cruising in
Mickey's car. It gave that feeling of sheer freedom and
independence. The budding teen beauties could roll the
windows down and let the whole world see who they
were.

Chris opened her knapsack hurriedly and took out
the small red and white package, and pulled out two
cigarettes. Once they were both lit, Chris took a monster
drag and held the smoke in dramatically. "Damn, I
needed that!" she exclaimed. "Have you made up your
mind about what you're doing your paper on?"

"Shit no! I still don't know. You know me. I always
wait until the last minute. You know, I guess I work
better under pressure. What are you going to do?"
Mickey always made excuses for postponing
assignments.

"Well, I figure if I do something about drug abuse
I've got a decent amount of references at hand and my
parents can help me some."

"Super. You always think of good things to write

about," Mickey said. She felt rather academically challenged compared to her astute companion who always beat deadlines.

"Why don't you write yours on 'Promiscuity in Your Teen Years'? You would certainly have a plethora of firsthand information on that subject," Chris suggested, trying to keep a straight face.

"Fuck you, girlfriend!" Mickey teasingly retorted.

"No, I think you've got me mixed up with somebody else."

Mickey laughed and mockingly sang "Some Kind of Wonderful." She had her first sex when she and Allen Carson had played in the woods one day when she had just turned thirteen. It was just a natural event. She showed him hers and he gladly showed her his and they sort of knew what they were supposed to do with each other. He watched her rub herself after he ejaculated, having only inserted his penis for a minute. It had been fun for Mickey, and she couldn't really see any harm in it. She was an only child and her mom and dad both worked, which gave her some degree of freedom. Her dad owned a small insurance brokerage firm and her mom was a dietitian at St. Ives Nursing Home. The entire family was very attractive. Mickey's looks were a sharp contrast to Chris's dark blond hair and freckles. Mickey had enormous green eyes that pierced at first sight and rich olive skin that didn't require make-up. She wore her almost-black hair in a severe blunt cut that ended at the tip of her ears. Mickey was considered gorgeous by both female and male students, along with some of the amorous faculty at Center Ridge High.

"Is your mom okay?" Mickey asked Chris cautiously.

"Why are you asking?" Chris answered after a lengthy pause.

"She looked a little tired and well, touchy. And sort of nervous. Your mom is always so chilled out and calm, but the other night at dinner she just didn't seem herself."

"I haven't talked about this because dad insisted it's sort of a 'private family thing.' I've really been worried about her. I'm not sure whether I'm embarrassed or just scared, but I think she's real close to having a breakdown. It might partially be because of her age or she's wondering who Dad's putting it to these days. I swear, my dad sure gets around!" Chris mused. "Well, anyway, he must be really worried about her, which is something he doesn't do very often. He told me and Paige to be very understanding and patient."

Mickey listened closely to her friend, not taking her eyes off the road. Chris explained the supposed intrusions, which no one else besides Clair attested to. When she filled Mickey in on the threatening letter, her friend's eyes darted back and forth.

"This is beginning to sound a little bit scary," Mickey uttered in disbelief.

"Next, look, I know it sounds silly, but she couldn't find a pair of her red panties she was going to wear to a dinner party the other night. The police came to investigate. And would you believe, she found them in her closet a couple of days later. Do you think the mystery was solved then?"

Mickey lit another cigarette directly after putting out her first one. She anticipated the grand conclusion.

"Not hardly! The panties really did look like someone

jerked off in them. I'm not kidding! Okay, now this is three times that the police have come to the house. The neighborhood probably thinks my parents are criminals. Are you getting the picture?"

Mickey nodded her head excitedly, "Shit, Chris, I had no idea that anything like this was going on. How are you able to sleep in that house?" She blew a stream of smoke from the corner of her mouth toward the open window.

"Well, up until now, Dad, Paige and I thought our mother was so overworked that she's been imagining most of these things. No one really did the dirty thing in her panties. The police said that it was just dried up dishwashing soap or something like that. Okay, so she checks the mail a few days later, and presto, a letter from some weirdo bastard who hates Jews. A real note. This is the really freaky part. It's done like the kidnappers do it when they send the ransom note. He or she, whoever, cut these letters out of books and magazines and pasted them together. Man, did she come apart then!"

"No kidding?"

"Hell yes. That letter clearly states she must die. I mean my mom must die. Talk about scaring the piss out of you. On top of that, he calls her a whore. Of all the people in the world I know, Mom should be the last one called that."

"What are the police doing?"

"Well, they are probably keeping a closer watch than we know about. Seems like there is always police driving by the house now."

"Damn, Chris, that's really freaky."

"Tell me about it."

"How come you didn't clue me in on this before? Aren't I your best friend?" Mickey again emphasized the danger Chris was in by staying at the house.

"Look, it's kind of hard to admit that your mom is freakin'. Then, when the death threat came, we all got pretty upset. That's why my mom looks so strung out."

"God, I'm so sorry," Mickey consoled with sincerity. "The police will find out who's doing this. Don't worry. They've always been able to stay on top of the drugs at school, haven't they? Hell, the druggies don't have too much of a chance here and hopefully this crazy bastard won't either." She threw the butt to the wind and felt the evening air chill her arm as they drove into the Center Ridge Mall's parking area.

Julia sat in her car in the shadows. She watched Martin get into a gold van that had been waiting for at least ten minutes, and leave from the darkness of the delivery entrance in the back of the hospital. She knew it, damnit, and it hurt like hell. That son of a bitch was seeing someone else. "Your ass is grass, big boy. This time, I've got you by the nuts." She put her car into drive and turned into the main parking lot and turned on her headlights. Julia felt it just might be time to let his wife know that her high and mighty husband was seeing someone else. He was now being unfaithful to both of them. When her shift ended, she would write Dr. Clair Weinstein a letter and enjoy every word of it.

Martin hated that Nancy was wearing perfume as he stepped into her van. It was always a dead giveaway, no matter how subtle or overpriced the shit was, he thought. Martin had met her in Mark Stern's office, and almost couldn't breathe because she was so beautiful. Her broad smile had instigated the attraction game. Her breasts were small and she was quite thin, but her ass was precariously shapely. Her lips looked like pieces of shiny red hard candy that stayed perfectly slick. Blondes normally didn't appeal to Martin but as Rocky eagerly approved this one, he simply would not decline. They were on their way to a small Italian restaurant in North Castle. Nancy had suggested it, and the timing couldn't have been better. Martin needed a break from all the chaos that was going on at home.

"Are you hungry, Doctor?" Nancy inquired with a wink. Yes, he certainly was. So was Rocky.

CHAPTER SEVEN

CHRIS AND CLAIR SAT ON THE SOFA TOGETHER in the den thumbing through magazines. They found two detailed articles on drug abuse from *Journal of Biochemistry* and a recent issue of *Proceedings of the National Academy of Sciences.* Chris was banking on the notion that her mother would translate all the studious terminology for her.

"How many references will you need?" Clair asked.

"At least five." Without fail, Chris planned on exceeding that number.

"Be sure and check with Sarah tomorrow. She might have put some of the old issues down in the basement. I know she takes them to the nursing home sometimes."

"I'll do that, and I'm also going to the library downtown this week. They've got a great reference file." She had also planned to interview a few students at school, and the drug rehab people had agreed to spend some time with her. She was usually stimulated by getting really involved in a project, and this one looked as though it could be particularly interesting.   Chris noticed in the warm glow of the lamp beside them that her mother looked almost like she used to, before the stress lines and dark circles. She thought she even looked pretty. It was a good time to discuss pressing matters.

"Mom, Kenny Weed asked me to go to the prom."

"I don't think I know him, do I?"

"No, I don't think so. He's new this year and is real quiet."

"Well, tell me about him." Both girls were always vague about who they were interested in, and this disappointed Clair. She thought of herself as a trusting and lenient parent.

"He's a little taller than me. He is kind of stocky, not much, just a little. His hair is dark and short and he has blue eyes. He is nice-looking, I guess. Yes, Mom, before you ask, he is a very good student. No tattoos or pierced ears."

Clair laughed. "That's good, darling, but that's not what I was curious about. I was only going to ask you what your answer was. Did you accept his invitation?"

"Sure. We get along great and have a lot in common. Oh, it's not a 'love connection' but he is fun and we have several classes together." Chris wasn't going to tell her mother that she and Kenny saw each other at the mall as often as possible and that he had already touched her breasts. His kisses were becoming more demanding. Most of her girlfriends were sexually active on some level. Maybe they weren't having real sex, but they were doing everything else. So far, Chris had chosen not to get into a compromising situation, and she hadn't gotten to the point of losing control. She really did not want to be sexually active yet. She already had her future mapped out and the lineup did not include an unwanted pregnancy or an authoritative boyfriend.

"I guess we need to think about a prom dress, don't we?"

Chris continued to hold the magazines. "Guess so."

"Why don't we go to the mall tomorrow night and look around. How much time do we have?"

"Plenty. It's not for three weeks. Can Mickey come with us?"

"I expected that she would." Clair enjoyed Mickey's company and found her to be a charming companion for Chris—even if it was obvious the girl didn't give a damn about school.

After class Josh slipped carefully up the ladder into his private place. His father had been quite temperamental earlier. Josh didn't make it rain, but Justin had sure taken it out on him with a hard whipping. Just because he couldn't work, he went on a rampage and terrorized the household. Josh carried a deep red bruise across his left cheek. This one had really made his head spin. He wasn't sure that he didn't black out for a second or two. He squeezed his eyes shut in attempt to clear his thoughts. Damn it, he always hated going to school with a red cheek. Everybody looked at him ridiculously, and his teachers asked him questions about his black eye or the bruise on his cheek. He would make up stories about falling out of a tree or walking into the door or getting in a fight. Josh was becoming a pro at churning out lies. On some days when he was sore and black and blue, he didn't go to school. He would hide in his safe place. Josh had discovered this corner of the top of the garage after another morning when his father had beaten the shit out of him. There was a partial floor that had been built out of scrap plywood overages from some of Justin's jobs. The Campbells used this part of their garage for storage. He had to be very careful because the plywood panels were not nailed down. It was a balancing act sometimes. Josh knew all the weak places that would not support him and always walked where he knew it was safe. Once he was up there, he could sit behind the boxes and never be found, providing no one saw him climb the ladder. He was damn careful about that. Josh had taken one of the bigger boxes and meticulously emptied it into other partially empty ones. He had taken that big box and turned it on its side facing the pitch of the roof. This protected him against any prying eyes. He loved the smell of his place, which was comprised of wood, tarpaper and old things that didn't have a use anymore. He liked the smell of oil and gas that would drift up once in a while too. Maybe it was a guy thing. Josh would share his secret place with James someday, but eleven was too young to harbor such privileged information. If someone threatened or tricked him, James would surely give in.

Josh hated the man that hurt them all so much. He had been making plans to leave for years, but his mother's sad, defenseless face always pulled him back. If he could just stop him from taking her downstairs after he and James were sent to bed. He couldn't understand or hear what his father was saying; it sounded a little like when he preached to them when they were bad. Josh heard his mom's soft cries and felt the vomit stirring in his stomach. Josh knew that he was doing it to her. That, he could tell. Why else would she cry out that way? That nasty old bastard was hurting her. Josh felt tears sting his eyes just thinking about it. He cried at night when it happened and he could cry in his secret place, where no one could see. His face throbbed in pain and bulged like the blood was just about to bust out of his skin.

"Someday Mama, I'm going to get you out of here. I swear. You too, James." Josh didn't know whom he was swearing to except himself. He snapped on his flash-light and opened his magazine to pages of bare bodies of women in all kinds of positions draped in furs, feathers and come-hither smiles.

Linda and James sat in the den watching "Wheel of Fortune." They tried to guess the phrase or puzzle before the contestants and sometimes they did. Linda stared blankly at the excited players, thinking about how upset she had been all day. Josh had gotten a bad beating. Justin hit those boys way too hard; however, he was the head of the family and she knew better than to question his authority. No, that would go against the Scriptures. Linda was already on thin ice and was not for one minute going to put herself in any deeper trouble than she was in already.

"Signed, sealed and delivered!" James yelled, and triumphantly threw his arms into the air as Vanna swirled in her long blue dress and turned the six E's.

"I believe you're right, son."

"Told ya! Told ya!"

That finished the round and the contestant won $15,000 and a chance to win a car.

"Looky there, James. See what you could've won if you was inside that TV," his mother encouraged.

"I don't want no dinky car. I'd rather have me a jet ski or a wave runner. Then me and Josh could go out to the lake and just race around."

Linda looked down at her boy sitting on the floor and knew he would never be allowed to go to the lake and ski. The only water sport their father would allow his boys was fishing. Even then, the boys never really enjoyed it because their daddy limited the fun. He was so strict. Seemed like they never did anything the right way, she thought. If a fish got away, they received a lecture on how the Lord took things away as a result of wrongdoing, so the boys were accused of sinning. She wondered what their lives would be like without Justin and his strict ways. "Oh dear Lord, I'm sorry for thinking such blasphemous thoughts. Justin is a good, hardworking man," she said to herself. She didn't feel very good. Linda figured that the pills were making her sick to her stomach. She'd take them anyway because she knew she could not go to the hospital. That just could not happen. She cringed at the thought of what Justin would do if he found out she had gone to a Jewish woman doctor and that she had touched her down there. Linda knew his wrath would be a whole lot worse than the Lord's.

Pat told Richard, the nervous contestant that the winning word was an occupation. The letters displayed below the blank spaces were R, S, T, N, and E. The clock ticked and Vanna turned over a T and an R. It was close but Richard correctly guessed that the word was "author."

Everyone yelled and Vanna turned over the remaining letters and Pat awarded Richard the keys to a red car. Linda and James watched the mustached young man jump up and down while looking at the audience. Soon a young woman and two older folks surrounded him. As they all jumped and hugged, brightly colored balloons and confetti fell around them.

"Got any homework, son?"

"Yes ma'am. I got a spellin' test tomorrow. I think I know all the words."

"I'll call them out to you and you can practice. Go get your book."

James spelled all but two perfectly. Linda circled the two he had missed. "All you got to do is study these two. You did real good. I suspect you get your good spellin' from your mama. I won more than one spellin' bee." She felt the pain again and reminded herself that she had to take one of her pills before going to bed.

"Mama, I'm about starved to death. Something sure smells good."

"Boy, you're always hungry. It's that beef stew y'all didn't eat up the other night. We'll eat soon as your daddy gets home. He went to the gas station and I suspect he'll be home directly. Do you know where your brother is?"

"Nope, but I'll go find him, Mama," and he dashed out with the screen door slamming behind him.

Josh found James first. He was feeling much better

than an hour before.

Linda washed the dishes after they had all eaten in silence. Justin had ushered Josh into the den for a talk.

"Son, we need to talk about your lessons."

"Yes sir."

"This here paper was in your book. Can you explain why there is a D on this arithmetic paper?"

"Yes sir."

"I'm listenin'," he claimed as he was undoing his belt. "Come on, son, talk to me."

Josh knew it wasn't going to do him any good. He saw his father's eyes turn into narrow slits and knew what was going to happen. The bastard was going to beat him again, no matter what.

"Daddy, I just didn't understand," he moaned as the first strike of the belt bit into his arm and shoulder. It almost rocked him off his feet.

"Please, Daddy, I don't know how to do . . ." Another cracking sound as the belt left its second red mark. This time he felt the wetness of blood running down his back.

Linda watched just like she always did. Oh, she knew he needed punishing, but did it have to be beatings? This was the second time in one day. She felt every pain Josh did, and wished Justin would just give her the whipping instead. She prayed to herself vehemently.

"Jesus, help him, please help him. Dear Lord, help us all."

It was Wednesday and Clair only had rounds to make. One of her patients had been admitted in ER.

After hemorrhaging all morning, her husband brought her in. Lisa Billings worked as a bank officer and was extremely active. She pursued a regular exercise program, ran a few miles every other day and played on a tennis team. By the time she walked into the small examining room, her vitals looked good and the hemorrhage was checked.

"Hello, Lisa. What happened?" Clair pushed the distraught woman's hair away from her face.

"Well, I really don't know. I thought I was about to start my period, but the cramps were really worse than usual. When I got up this morning for my run, I started flooding, and it just wouldn't let up."

"We are going to need to run a few tests after I examine you."

Everything appeared normal, but the bleeding had come on too suddenly.

"I'd like to schedule you for a D and C in the morning. It's best if we admit you now, and give your body some time to rest since the bleeding is checked."

On the way home Clair was feeling ravenous. No wonder; it was almost one o'clock and her morning coffee was long gone. She would fix herself a sandwich and catch up on some of her personal correspondence. Then she would have the afternoon to help Chris look for more reference material for her term paper. Later, she and the girls would go to the mall to look at prom dresses.

After checking her messaging service, Clair sat in the kitchen nibbling on a peach scone while talking with Sarah. She had liked this robust woman from the moment they met. Her daughter was expecting another baby, and Clair shared her delight.

"Doctor said it could be twins. Lordy, Dr. Clair, if that were to happen, Amanda would really have her hands full with the boys and all. You know how active those boys are now. Whew!" Sarah roared, shaking her head while she ran the iron over the skirt on the ironing board.

"Oh, Sarah, let's hope it's not twins. My personal philosophy has been that one is enough. Being a physician, I had enough trouble balancing my life with one baby at a time and I did not breastfeed. Both girls fortunately were healthy as little horses when I delivered. Oh, they had the normal little ear and throat problems that are inherent with infants. We all experience these things but I had a devil of a time just trying to make everything work out. I did take a short leave, and I did have a nanny, who was a tremendous help."

"Did you not want to breastfeed?" The old-fashioned sweetheart would surely go into one of her spiels but Clair didn't mind. She was glad for the company.

"Sure I did, but my milk was not good. I could make the baby but I couldn't feed it. Thank heavens for premixed formulas."

"Oh, I know about that. My daughter, Tonya couldn't feed her boys, neither one of them. She said it was a lot easier, but she said that she sure missed out on that part of being a mama," Sarah said. "I fed all of mine. I was a real milk factory. Look at me now." She looked down at her own large breasts. "Before Mr. Lyles passed, he used to tell me that a woman is in full bloom when she is my size. God bless him. He always made me feel pretty. He didn't do it in what you might call fancy ways, but he sure did it."

"By the way, Sarah, did you put any magazines in the basement?" Clair changed the subject unintentionally.

"Sure did.   Weren't enough to take to the nursing home so I just stuck them in a box down there.   It's marked real good. I wrote 'magazines' on the top," she explained.

CHAPTER EIGHT

CLAIR AND CHRIS WENT DOWNSTAIRS INTO the basement to look through the boxes. There were shelves and several rooms that had collected many relics and special memorabilia from upstairs. Old lamps, books, papers that might be needed someday, hat boxes, bags of old clothing, and boxes of special tchotchkes were scattered about begging to be put in some sort of order. The mystery boxes probably held collectibles from the girls' childhood. Clair had not been down there for a long time. It always made her feel a bit uneasy and she could not pinpoint why. The overhead light dimmed by cobwebs gave them adequate light for their search. Even when Martin had his shop down there, Clair never made it a regular place to visit. It was his outlet, after all.

They discovered the magazines and returned to the den. Clair and Chris became absorbed in the heap of erudite publications that offered possibilities for a paper on drug abuse. Neither one spoke for a while until Chris suggested making something to eat. Clair agreed to have a surprise treat as she continued to thumb through the pages.

"What do you want to drink, Mom?"

"Do we have a raspberry soda left?"

After a moment of searching the fridge, Chris announced that there was one sugary, tart can left. She didn't know of other parents who were medical practitioners and such enthusiasts of anything sugary, alcoholic and caffeinated. The pair drank enough coffee to fill a kona bean plantation.

Clair opened another journal. She had looked through the indexes and there was an article on how the importation of drugs had increased, despite the new technology of detection. She wondered if this was a government plot. At that time, she hadn't noticed the two tiny holes cut out on the pages she had been thumbing through.

"Okay, Mom, time out for a snack." Chris presented her with a plate of Ritz Crackers and peanut butter and a frosted mug of raspberry soda.

"Eat, I'll get mine. I changed my mind and fixed myself a peanut butter and jelly. It's hard to smell peanut butter without eating it! I wrapped one up for Dad too. I owed him for the last batch I finished off." She retrieved her sandwich and a can of Coke. Chris was bored with the research and eager for a shopping spree. She was also anxious to disclose the name of her "mystery prom date" to Mickey.

The trio roamed the mall and visited most of the specialty shops and department stores that carried formal wear. Chris and Mickey tried on dress after dress, giggling while Clair offered colorful remarks about each garment. Neither one made a decision. Mickey and Chris discussed how each one had looked in particularly pretty—and slinky—dresses, and shrieked theatrically about the very unflattering ones.

Clair and Chris said goodnight to Mickey at her door and drove home. They were both tired and didn't return to the den. Chris went to bed and Clair headed for the kitchen to fix a cup of jasmine tea. A box of animal crackers would be a fitting accompaniment, she thought. Clair saw that the sandwich Chris had fixed for her father was still in the refrigerator untouched. Martin had not been home yet.

Josh lay in his bed and stared at the ceiling, feeling the pain of every red strip across his back and legs. They all throbbed in unison. He wanted sleep to come and relieve him. How much more of this could he take? His dad had been on a real spree lately. Why didn't the bastard understand that he didn't know what in the world he was supposed to be doing in his math class? He got lost in all the fractions and "numerical sentences" the teacher gleefully chatted about. Besides, how much of all that math shit was he going to need anyway? After all, he knew how to add and subtract, multiply and divide.

In the semi-darkness he could see Jesus' body hanging on the cross. His parents had hung this picture over his chest of drawers to remind him that Jesus had died for all their sins. Josh hated the picture. It reminded him of pain. In the dark sometimes the head on the crucified figure became his father's. Only then did he like the picture. If he ever had a son, the kid would never be treated like his father treated him. Never! He couldn't stay there much longer. And, he wouldn't. Even if he had to hustle in the streets or beg for a bus ticket somewhere, Josh promised himself.

Josh didn't go to school that next morning. He got dressed, picked at his breakfast, gathered his books, and said goodbye to his parents. He followed the path to the barn at the crossroads. If any of the guys skipped school, they would hide out at Benson's barn for a while. Josh sat alone in the shabby structure and waited for a couple of hours for his house to empty. He knew his dad would be at work and his mother would be going to the church to meet with those other women who printed up the programs for Sunday service or worked in that secondhand store. After a cigarette and a hot Coke that Ronnie had stowed away in an old sealed plastic paint bucket, he headed home to retreat in his spot. He discovered that Ronnie didn't go to school frequently either and he wondered where he was that afternoon. They were two of a kind, he and Ronnie. They had jerked off together to see who could do it the farthest. They had both stolen candy and chips from the Mini-Mart. That mean old lard barrel, Mrs. Green, had almost caught them on an occasion or two. She must have had eyes in all that kinky white hair or maybe there were hidden cameras all over her store.

The Campbells' garage faced the path from the woods, and he could get there without being seen from the house. As he climbed the ladder balancing his way

back to his box, he felt every whelp from the previous
night's beating. Josh had his Walkman, his *Secret Lady*
for "adults only" and enough detective magazines to
keep him occupied for the afternoon. When he wanted
to pee he just did it in the big blue Maxwell House coffee can. When it got full he would pour it into the bushes through the open eaves. He also had his flashlight, a
few cans of Coke and several bags of chips. Josh never
knew when he would have to hide for a long time. If he
needed a blanket, he could always retrieve one from the
box that contained old torn and soiled ones. Josh
already had two pillows in case he wanted to take a nap.
It also made his little place quite comfortable. He settled in, and even though the surface was not as soft as
his bed, the safety he felt improved his spirits. The box
had its own way of being comfortable. For a while, he
would be safe in a place that didn't exist to anyone but
him. He only had to wait one more year before he could
get his driver's license. He would get it, despite his
father. Josh knew he had to start planning for his future.
He needed a job after school and he would look for one
the first of the week. He could hide his money in one of
the boxes, and when he saved enough, he would get his
mother and James the hell out of there. In fact, he
would drive them to California or Alaska and enjoy
every damned mile. Boy, would his dad be pissed! And
who would care? The three of them would be free. He
would take care of his mama and his little brother, and
the old bastard would finally suffer for the pain he had
caused them. "I just hate him," Josh gritted through his
teeth. Josh envisioned their new lives out west, where
his mother would be healthy and happy. He was already

feeling better. Dreaming of a new beginning free of cruelty was very healing.

In a downstairs Sunday school room, Linda sat at a table folding clothes and sorting them by size and gender. Jacob and Christina Fincher had started The Temple of Jesus Christ Thrift Store. Two days a week Linda would meet with other sisters of the church to organize items that had been donated. Justin strongly disapproved, as did the rest of the brotherhood.

"Won't be sellin' to nothin' but niggers," Justin had ranted. "I'm tellin' ya, just niggers. I won't be donating any of my things for some jumbo to wear around town and neither will you, and you can damn sure count on that. You hear me?" he had threatened.

Linda knew in her heart that charity was something she could not abandon. There were folks out there who needed things. Little kids needed decent clothes to go to school in, and have coats to keep them warm when it got cold. Wasn't it a sin not to be charitable? Linda even cited a passage from Justin's precious Bible in defense of donating clothes to that family from Porterdale: "Therefore take heed to yourselves and to all the flock, among which the Holy Spirit has made you overseers, to shepherd the church of God which he purchased with his own blood." Acts 20:28 was not convincing enough to "aid niggers," the stubborn man had said. He didn't even care that the family of seven had been sleeping in one room and had shared torn blankets from a dumpster.

"Linda, are you all right? You're lookin' a bit peaked." Lillian Marsh, a large-boned woman of about forty-five or so, asked her friend with sincere concern.

Linda didn't hear that kind of tenderness very often anymore. She tended to be frightened of anyone knowing anything about the family's personal business. She tried to stay strong, but the tears welled up in her eyes and then ran down her cheeks in a flood.

"I'm sorry if I upset you," Lillian said and she leaned over to hug her. "I'm so sorry."

Linda continued to cry. "I guess that I must be going through my change." Although she didn't have the slightest understanding of what the "change" really meant, it was the easiest excuse.

"Are you sure that's all that's abothern' you? You know that I won't tell nobody and we can pray together for His help." Lillian raised her right arm over her head, and shut her eyes to pray. "Praise Jesus, I know you will help this sister, your devoted daughter." Linda sat in the chair beside her and held her hand.

"Blessed Lord, take care of this hurtin' member of your flock." Lillian's eyes opened and looked upward, "She needs you real bad, precious Jesus. You are the giver of life and we are all sinners that must feel your wrath at times, but Sister Linda here is a kind gentle woman, who is hurtin' now, and she loves you Lord. Help me to be your instrument so I can be a good and trusting friend and help her pain go away. Amen."

"Thank you Lord, amen." Linda said quietly lowering her head again. She wiped her face and looked at her friend. "Thank you, Lillian. Sometimes I just don't know where to turn. I mean, I've really sinned."

Lillian continued to hold her friend's hand. "You sound like you've killed somebody or committed adultery."

"No Lillian, you ain't helpin' no criminal or adulteress, but it's too private to talk about. Justin told me I let Satan in and I've been contaminated, and besides that, I've not been feeling very well lately."

"I know you ain't been well. Looks to me like you're just plain gettin' skinny. I can see it in your face that you don't feel good and you've been draggin' around for a while now. Linda, how can I help you? You already know I'll pray for you." Lillian stood and put her hands on her friend's shoulder.

"Thank you." Linda felt a little more strength knowing that she had partially confided in her friend. She couldn't come out and tell her about her real sin. She couldn't tell anybody. She would be too embarrassed and besides, talking about sex was a complicating task. She had never even discussed the subject with her own husband. Justin would be furious with her if she did. It was sinful. After all, she had acted like a harlot on that ominous night. Justin was quick to cast judgement by spouting out a verse from Revelations bitterly:

> And the ten horns which you saw on the beast,
> these will hate the harlot make her desolate
> and naked and burn her with fire!

Linda had cowered in absolute fear until her sweaty husband rolled off of her.

"Linda, would you like to have some coffee?" Lillian asked, hoping the invitation would shift the mood.

Linda accepted gratefully, determined to get Justin's raspy voice out of her head.

Linda unlocked her kitchen door. It was time to get

dinner started. She felt a little better "down there." She laid the paper and mail on the counter and thought of Lillian and how kind she had been to her. There wasn't anyone she could truly talk to but the Lord. She pulled frozen pork chops from the freezer and set them on the counter by the sink, then she took out the orange sack of potatoes, anxious to get started on the routine of peeling them. Linda thought of her boys and how the Lord had asked Abraham to give his son to prove his love. It was only a test and God didn't take him because Abraham had been willing to do it. Had she sacrificed Josh and James in some way already? Their beatings, her cleansing and his judgment served as that despicable offering. In reality, was it the Lord's decree or Justin's?

The birds recited music for Clair. She loved this time of year. The puffy clouds along the tree line beyond the house were comforting, and the sky was yellow and blue. It would soon be summer. She could feel the season and smell it.

It was too beautiful to stay inside. She breezed through the kitchen and den, grabbing her mail, *USA Today* and cup of coffee to take outside to the brick patio connected to the breakfast room. She settled herself in the old lounge and relaxed. The yellow bug light was already on, even though she still had sufficient daylight. The landscape around their home had not changed much over the years. The girls' play area, swing set and sandbox had been long gone, but Clair could still recall the girly squeals from that part of the lawn. Down the slope of the well-manicured lawn was Martin's new workshop. Years ago his brother Sid had advised him to take up a hobby. It would help him "live longer." Martin purchased a few power tools and set up a workshop in the basement. Despite the electrical enhancements and state-of-the-art dust collecting system, it still caused power outages in the old house, not to mention the dust and noise that could not be contained downstairs. Martin didn't have an abundance of time, but on weekends, she would awake to the faint sound of the radial arm saw. Even with the one-story and lots of woods between them, the antiquated piping allowed sounds to creep around the house.

Clair opened her bills and set them aside. In the middle of the stack was a small violet envelope addressed to her. She opened it and unfolded a very pretty piece of lacy stationery. She could smell the lavender. How pleasant, she thought. Clair focused on the neatly typed message:

Dear Dr. Weinstein:

You don't know me but I have respected and admired you from afar for a very long time.

I know you must be a fine mother and a wonderful servant of your community. I never hear anything detrimental about your character. Some time ago, I met this man and he did something very cruel and painful to me. He started seeing someone else. I just happened to catch him. I was truly devastated by it but I will recover. I think it might be a different story with your husband. If you want to catch him you might want to check the delivery entrance at the Center Ridge Hospital at night. The only reason that I am writing to you is that I have also felt the pain of deception. Please forgive my awkwardness, but I am very sorry this has happened to you.

The sender had signed as "Someone who shares your pain."

All the reverie Clair had felt earlier fled with the afternoon sun. Clair sat dry-eyed, staring past the trees that would soon be loaded with plums and figs. She heard the sound of the evening doves but it was not soothing. Clair held her knees close to her and became very small in the yellow light. She had never wanted to know. Not really, and now, she didn't know if the validation even mattered.

Justin smelled sour from sweat. He had worked hard in the heat. He meticulously placed his tools in the shiny lock-up in the back of his truck. His tools were his livelihood. He stood beside his truck talking to Curtis Watson, an old man that often helped him on his construction jobs. It was just about dark and Justin didn't usually work this late. "Days are gettin' longer. Better start lookin' at my watch," he said to Curtis. "We're almost done with this addition, buddy. It's looking mighty fine if I have to say so myself."

"Yes sir, it sure does. I bet we'll be done by the middle of next week, cleanup and all," the old man responded with pride.

"I wonder what my wife is fixin' for dinner," Justin said feeling his hunger. "She better not have any of that box stuff or foreign mess. You can't even tell what you're eatin'."

Curtis rolled his eyes in disgust. "No sir, it could be dog or cat. Sure is hard to train those women with all that stuff from Satan they see and hear on TV getting in their brains all day long."

"I know," Justin agreed. "I bought that thing so I could watch the news at night and see the wrestlin' matches on the weekends. I like some of the TV preachers, but not many. Some of those guys sure do get caught doin' some stuff. I know it's a plot. Too many niggers and Jews on nowadays. They own it all, don't forget that, buddy."

After the seven-mile trek home, Justin pulled up in the garage and walked into the house. As he passed the ligustrum bushes, he smelled something rancid. He stopped briefly. "Are those boys pissin' in the bushes? Got two bathrooms in the house and they gotta piss outside." He'd find out who did it. Just maybe both of them needed a little bruisin'.

The aroma in the kitchen was a welcome contrast.

"Linda, where are you?"

"I'm in the laundry room, I'm foldin' clothes. Supper's almost done."

"What are we havin'?"

"Pork chops, peas, mashed potatoes, and sweet tea!" she yelled from the laundry room.

"Where are the boys?"

"Josh is doin' homework and James is watchin' TV."

Linda joined him in the kitchen. He was sitting down at the pre-set table.

"Why is James watchin' TV? Don't he have studies to do? I don't like those boys watchin' so much of that mess. Full of Satan. I'm tellin' you, Linda. James!" Justin hollered.

"Yes sir," James answered.

"I want you lookin' at your school books. Turn that mess off," Justin demanded.

"Yes sir," James answered obediently and turned off the cartoon he had been watching, and went to his room.

Linda followed James down the hall with the clothes-basket, quietly urging him to read something—any-thing—to keep peace in the family. James obeyed imme-diately. He skimmed his geography book until he was called to dinner.

"Dear Heavenly Father, thank you for what we are about to receive. Keep our lives filled with you, dear Lord. Protect us from Satan and all of his works. Help me to guide this family into your glory. Amen."

They ate their dinner in silence. James wondered how many times his father said "Lord" or "Satan" in one day. Justin eyed the boys closely, wondering which one was peeing in the bushes like a pig.

Justin ate entirely too much and just wanted to plop down in his chair in time for the evening news. He was too full and tired to care anymore about whose fault it was; he would approach the subject later. Snores soon came to the heavy man in the recliner. He had only watched the evening news for five minutes.

Josh rushed to his room and James sat beside his mama, quietly watching crime rage over the planet via satellite.

Martin fell beside Nancy in an exhausted heap. He

had really worked up a sweat and Nancy's golden hair was matted and wet. She, too, gasped for air while recovering from their wild adventure in ecstasy. Martin pulled her to him with both of his arms and held her closely. He desperately wanted to fall asleep just like he was, but the red numbers on her clock read 9:15. He kissed her and tasted the salt on her skin. She was delicious.

"Do you really have to go?" Nancy purred.

"Yes, my beauty, I must get home before I cause too much of a stir."

He stepped into the shower under the cold water that jolted his senses. "Whew!" he cried out. "Nothing wakes you like a cold shower." Martin scrubbed vigorously to remove any trace of sex, blond hair or perfume.

He slid into his own bed a little after 10:20. He felt wonderful. Chris and Clair had both retired. They must have gotten tired of looking through magazines. He had a few in his office desk drawer. He would try to remember to bring them home in the morning.

Clair heard Martin come in, but she just lay in bed staring into the darkness. Why couldn't she just either get used to this or end the marriage? They had been together for so many years, and reshaping her life would be painstaking. Damn it, she had never really wanted to know about his extramarital activities. Not from some well-meaning sharer of pain or anyone else, she thought. How many times did she deserve to be hit between the eyes with a two-by-four? The letter had not been a giant revelation.

Linda sat in the den idly watching the twenty-five-inch screen. The white-haired attorney from Atlanta was solving the puzzle of the murder of a business executive who was on the verge of a divorce. Justin didn't move. He just snored with his eyes shut and his mouth open. She decided not to disturb him.

She undressed quietly and slipped into bed. Linda knew she was getting better because the pain in her vagina was not so bad now. It was sort of a dull ache and it didn't sting. Linda rolled onto her side, pulled the sheet over her shoulder and stared at the small figurines on the dresser. The security light from outside made them look like a little circus of characters that could be alive and talking to one another.

"Precious Jesus, my boys Josh and James need your help to grow up to be good Christian boys. Jesus, please protect them. I'm not askin' for anything for myself now, just the boys. Look out for my boys. I can't hardly stand to see them gettin' beatings. Dear Lord, they're just little boys. I know Josh is strong-willed, but inside he is good and I know you gotta see that."

Morning came, and Justin stirred in his chair to the cast of "Good Morning America." He sat up and felt completely cramped. He slept in the den all night. He wondered why Linda hadn't prompted him up to go to bed. Justin found her in the bathroom brushing her teeth.

"Why didn't you wake me up last night? I slept in that cramped chair all night."

"Justin, I tried, " she lied. "You was just too tired, I reckon."

"I ain't going to be worth a whip today." He was mad at her, but he let it go. Justin showered, shaved and inspected his refection in the mirror. His hairline was receding and his broad square face was showing wrinkles. Justin squinted his eyes and wondered if he was beginning to look wiser as well as older; he liked the way he looked. He slapped on his Aqua Velva and got dressed. The smell of bacon accelerated his routine. Justin was damned hungry. Linda had breakfast ready when everyone stormed into the kitchen. The Campbell family sat to an ample breakfast of bacon, eggs, sweet milk, and canned biscuits. Justin said the blessing, and they ate for a while in silence.

"Which one of you boys is peein' in the bushes by the garage? Smells like a toilet out there," Justin grunted.

"I did Daddy," Josh spoke up all too fast. He had just dumped that can of pee the day before. "I couldn't wait. I was on the way home from school and like to have not made it home. It was the first place I could go without anybody seein' me."

"You best go before you leave school or stop at the Mini-Market. They got a toilet. I ain't goin' to have you killin' my bushes. You hear, son?" He spoke to Josh in that voice that usually preceded a beating.

"Yes sir. I'm sorry, Daddy." Josh woke up in a horrible mood and he had already fantasized about retaliating if the old man made a move for his belt.

Justin rose from the table mumbling, "I better not be smellin' no pee out by that garage anymore. I just better not."

They heard the sound of his pickup fade away, and all drew a sigh of relief.

Linda's day would be full. After her church work she was supposed to go to Dr. Clair's. She was afraid not to go. Her appointment was at one o'clock. This would give her time to gather her thoughts and face the prying doctor again. It was becoming harder and harder to look at that woman's face and not blurt out what was really happening to her. Linda wondered if anyone would really believe her anyway. She was close to confiding in Preacher Clower, but doubted he would help her in any way. He would surely brand her as a daughter of the devil.

CHAPTER NINE

ONE OF CLAIR'S PATIENTS HAD LEFT THE hospital. Just walked out. She was Mary Louise Crandall, a retired waitress in her mid-seventies, who some said was far from being mentally stable. Poor old thing, Clair mused, how did she ever pull off such a crazy trick? Night shift would be held responsible. Once in a great while a patient would slip out of the hospital without anyone detecting them but not very often as security was very tight.

Clair preferred her morning rounds. As she walked past the quickly moving nurses, aids and cleaners she felt the energy of the beginning shift. The large food cabinets were still in the hallways soon to be taken back to the kitchen. She smelled what was left of eggs, wheat toast and fruit juice. Martin was probably still in OR. This time of the day Clair was usually able to have one-on-one time with her patients, without the intrusion of family and visitors. Despite the commotion over Mrs. Crandall, her visits were brief and pleasant.

As Clair stepped into her clinic, Carla was evidently in rare form. She looked bright and exuberant. "I made it, Dr. Clair! I hit that damn goal. You are looking at one hundred and nine pounds."

"Congratulations! Carla, that is terrific. Maybe you could teach me something about self-discipline."

"The last five were the hardest. Absolutely the hardest! Charles and I celebrated last night. I don't know if you've noticed your own body, but you are losing weight too, Dr. Clair." Carla's observation was scrupulous.

"I suppose, but it's not self-imposed. To be very frank, it's been the hardest weight loss I've ever had to experience," she laughed ruefully.

Clair completed her busy morning schedule, briefly remembering she had received that stupid letter that revealed Martin's adultery. She had allowed herself to become vulnerable again. She knew better. After all, it was nothing new. She wasn't even going to acknowledge the damn thing. It just wasn't that important anymore.

A little after noon, a plain bagel and coffee became lunch and she made a call to check her patient's conditions at General. Maybe there had been news on the missing patient.

"Dr. Clair, Mrs. Crandall turned up at her sister's very early this morning. She's all right, but a little disoriented. Her sister is bringing her back after she cleans her up. Seems as though she got dirty in her escape adventure last night. She told her sister she had to break out because she was going to be 'executed' in the morning."

"Executed? Where did she come up with that? I am

not giving this patient anything that could cause hallucinations. I've heard of my care as being a devil to deal with sometimes, but this is the first time anyone has ever referred to it as a death sentence." Clair couldn't help smiling. She knew Mary Crandall as a sweet quiet lady. She had seemed sharp as a tack and had not given any evidence of dementia.

"Where do people think up such things? Well, Dr. Clair, we'll get everything squared away," Mrs. Jenkins said. "We'll go ahead and start the test you ordered when she gets here."

As she finished her call to Greg Shears in psychiatry, urging him to evaluate Mrs. Crandall, Carla peeked in. "Dr. Clair, there is a very nice-looking man out here to see you. Says he is an old friend."

Clair stood up and straightened herself. Normally she would have asked who it was but today a surprise would be appreciated.

Her breath caught thickly in her throat as she encountered her treasured friend. "Dave! My God, you look wonderful. How are you? When did you get here?"

He held her and tears stung her eyes.

"Whoa! I'm sorry, I am so damn glad to see you," as she pulled away. "What a wonderful surprise! Aren't you here a little early?"

"Clair, you never change. Always asking questions faster than I can answer. I flew in last night, and no, I'm not here early. I have another meeting with Ben Coffer, your illustrious administrator, and was hoping to see you and the family."

"That's great!" Clair was clearly elated as Carla stood

next to them curiously.

"How's Martin and the girls?"

"The girls are great, and Martin, well, you know Martin. He is still Martin."

"Sorry Clair, I had thought he might have straightened out."

"Look, we'll talk about it this evening. I've got a house full of ladies out there, each with something that needs to be seen to. Why don't we meet at Sculley's around eight? Can you do that?" Clair asked anxiously. Surely he would not decline her invitation. "It's a cute little place off the interstate on exit twenty-six. You can see the sign from the freeway. You can't miss it. It's north of the interchange, if that makes any sense to you."

He smiled warmly at her. "I'll manage I'm sure." His large hands held her shoulders and he kissed her cheek and left. Dave Corn was back and he couldn't have come at a better time. He even smelled the same. Clair reveled in the masculine scent all day.

She picked up her charts and saw her first two patients' standard biannual exams. Both of the two women were over forty and in relatively good health. Nothing was visibly abnormal. The next chart she took from the door slot gave her concern. Clair hoped this patient had improved severely. Carla was already there taking her blood pressure and temperature.

"Hello, Linda."

She smiled, "Dr. Clair, I do feel so much better. I don't know what was in them pills, but they sure made me get better. I didn't forget one time." She knew she hadn't had a cleansing either since her last exam.

"That is very good news!" Dr. Clair beamed with a genuine smile.

Dave was waiting for her in a booth in the back of Sculley's. The place was charming and unquestionably romantic. Music from the sixties softly played and occasionally an outburst of laughter could be heard. The lighting was gold, which gave the old wood decor a dark rich semblance. Sculley's looked very much like an old English pub; only the costumes of the characters were out of place.

He saw her and stood. "I ordered you a Manhattan. I hope you still drink them."

"I haven't had one in a very long time. Sounds just wonderful, but you might have to drive me home," Clair said.

"That would not be a problem." Dave noticed the lines in her face and her eyes that still sparkled with energy. She was still the same Clair, who had always excited him with her brilliance and sensuality. He reached for her hand. "I'm so glad to see you. I didn't realize how much I needed this."

"Me too. Life has been a bit crazy lately, but it's nothing we can't handle."

"What is it, Clair?" He was the same altruistic knight in shining armor he had always been—perfectly ready to aid those in need.

"Oh, some Jesus freak is playing mind games with me. I don't know whether he or she believes that I perform abortions or it's just the fact that I am Jewish. Hell, I don't know!" She smiled at him, and already feeling the effects of the alcohol, left her hand in his

comfortably.   Clair was more concerned with his
traumatic experience than the damned stalker.
"How are you?"

"Well, it's been a hard year. I tried to stay at
Moreland General, but it just carried far too many
memories. Life was moving right along. Barbara and I
were getting ready to send Sandra to Smith College.
Then I turned around and I was alone. They didn't exist
anymore. I didn't believe the state patrol when they
came to the house to tell me there had been a crash in
North Georgia and that my daughter and wife had not
survived. I just wasn't able to handle it. I took a leave
and spent some time with my parents. When I went back
I realized I really needed a change," Dave spoke with
conviction. He had been through a terrible time but
with the swig of his drink, he smiled and reverted the
conversation back to her. "So Clair, please, back to you!
You can't possibly take threats lightly. What exactly has
this freak done?"

Of course she wasn't taking the situation lightly; she
just wanted one solid night of abandoning the subject.
"Here's to your new beginnings," Clair toasted, gently
disregarding further discussion. They held their glasses
together.

"And your problems solved," he responded, and they
both drank.

Clair couldn't remember a Manhattan tasting so
good. The bartender had done it exactly right. The taste
of the drink brought back endearing memories. She
looked at her old friend with fondness. Even though
they had been better friends than lovers, at this moment,
the intimacy excited her.

Dave finally offered her a menu. "What are you in the mood for tonight?" He smiled and allowed the question to sound a little leading.

She returned the smile and opened the menu feeling a little flushed. Clair suggested a chicken dish and simmered potatoes, curtailing the recommendation with a wink. She turned her eyes to the menu and searched for the healthy and less fattening entrees. The night would be good, and she refused to let a huge meal deter her from making it last as long as she could.

On the way home, Clair was content and a little lightheaded. She blared her favorite jazz station, wondering if Martin was home yet.

At eleven o'clock Linda walked down the hall to the bathroom. She turned the shower on and felt the stinging of the water as soon as it ran down between her legs. Her face contorted in pain. There was semen mixed with blood. She remembered Justin's words earlier that evening—another fitting passage from Galatians in evaluation of her deeds. Linda wondered if God ever judged Justin or urged him to make specific references to the Scriptures.

> I say then: Walk in the spirit, and you shall not fulfill the lust of the flesh. For the flesh lusts against the spirit, and spirit against the flesh; and these are contrary to one another, so that you do not do the things you wish. But if you are led by the spirit, you are not under the law. Now the works of the flesh are evident, which are: adultery, fornication, uncleanness, licen-

> tiousness, idolatry, sorcery, hatred con-
> tentions, jealousy, outbursts of wrath, selfish
> ambitions, dissensions, and heresies.

Linda regretted that she had cried out, but the pain was unbearable. She had tried so hard to be quiet. Here we go again, Linda thought helplessly. She applied medicine on it and swallowed the last three pills. Her thoughts were not of shame this time. She was angry and humiliated. The whole ceremony was very demeaning. She tried to wash all her bad feelings from her body. Linda heard Justin come into the bedroom and shut the door. He strode into the bathroom and stood at the sink with his penis and testicles draped into the sink to rinse them off. After he had splashed them with the warm water he scrubbed them with bar soap, then he briskly dried as if he had just disinfected himself. The large hairy man disappeared into their bedroom and Linda was left to finish her shower in privacy. His intrusion irritated her.

"Hurry up in there, Linda," he ordered from their bed.

She didn't want to hurry. Linda would shower in there until he was snoring, even if she had to stand in ice-cold water.

Josh wiped at his tears and tasted the repugnancy in his mouth. He heard the water in their bathroom now, but he had previously heard his father preaching and his mother sobbing. He thought he had heard her cry out several times. He should have gotten up and helped his mother. "I'm sorry Mama. I'm so sorry," Josh stammered and turned his face into his pillow. He screamed silently into the foam particles, "I hate you, you bastard! I hate you!"

"Dave Corn is here.   He came by the office yesterday," Clair told Martin over morning coffee.

"I heard. Sorry I didn't get to see him. How is that rascal anyway?" Martin asked over his newspaper.

"Well, I think he looks great, considering. I'm going to show him the Raven Hills area tomorrow."

"You know, Clair, we are so fortunate to have the two wonderful girls we have. Maybe things in the past have not always been perfect between us, but I think we've pretty well worked that out, don't you?"

Clair wondered what he meant by the pronouncement. Was her husband being a little territorial or perhaps showing a bit of jealousy?

"Sure, Martin," she said without too much sincerity. "We had better get going."

Clair thought about Dave all day. She felt giddy. His easy dimpled smile was the same. His hair was almost white now and a bit thinner; he certainly looked older but he was still a very attractive man.

Nothing bothered or complicated her day.   Carla even commented, "Dr. Clair, you've been smiling all day."

She had indeed been smiling. How many years had it been since she felt like this? She wasn't even hungry at lunch. Instead she ate an apple and went over a few of her patients' charts.

That evening she would help Chris with her paper. Paige had called and proclaimed: "I'm coming home this weekend. Mystery meat number thirty-seven had been served three times this week and I am going through withdrawal for a home-cooked meal!"   Paige had become much closer since she moved away.   Clair was probably the same when she was her age.   Before she knew it, it was time to get in her car and head to the hospital to make rounds.   Her missing patient had been safely returned.   Her sister had brought her in, and at the present time, she refused any medical treatment. They would determine what to do after a psychiatric work-up.   Clair had seen one too many mercy killers on TV exposes, and at Mrs. Crandall's age, there was no telling what she was contemplating.   When she finished seeing her patients, Clair would welcome time at home. She knew Chris would entertain them with her school stories and class evaluations, and she was all too excited about spending more time with Dave.

Martin was busy in the kitchen when she got home. "I thought I'd cook tonight.   I haven't done this in quite a while.   I don't want to lose my touch."   He smiled warmly.   "We are having broiled yellow fin tuna, your favorite, romaine salad, and a 'perfectly chilled' Chardonnay, as you would say."

"Aren't you a sweetheart," she said with a smile. "Where's Chris?"

"She is eating her dinner in the food court at the mall."

"Again?   Oh well, I was looking forward to her company this evening.   I'm helping her with her paper."

"Oh yes, I remember.   I was going to bring some material home from the hospital and I keep forgetting."

They ate dinner by candlelight and Claude Debussy's

Tarantelle Styrienne.

"Well, how was it?" Martin asked shyly.

"Not too bad for someone who only does this once in a while," Clair said. "Just kidding, Martin. It was absolutely delicious." They smiled simultaneously at each other.

"Let's get this cleaned up. I want to help our daughter collate some articles when she gets home," Clair said as she started stacking the dishes and blowing out the candles.

Martin helped her with the cleanup and they chatted about car repairs, Chris's birthday and Paige's weekend visit.

When everything had been cleared away, Clair returned to the den to the small stack of magazines that she and Chris had brought up from the basement. She took a pad of yellow Post-it notes from the drawer beside her, figuring Chris would be home soon. She heard the water upstairs. Martin was in the shower.

Settled comfortably on the sofa, Clair marked the pages on one magazine and picked up another. As she turned the pages, she passed ads for "new technology in sound" and "how to expand the memory on a computer." And the issue of "clearing up skin problems" had gotten undoubtedly popular these days, Clair thought. She noticed small holes cut from the text. Clair opened another magazine. It was hole-less. She looked through another. The next inspection revealed four cutouts. Clair didn't look anymore. She just sat and stared at the rows of neatly lined books that filled the wall across from her. It appeared that her threatening letter might have been composed right there in the house, from her very own magazines. It just didn't make sense. No one in her family would have sent an anti-Semitic hate letter to her. Sarah? It was inconceivable. This diamond of a lady had been with them for years. Old Henry? Sure, he was of German descent, but he wouldn't even think to harm anyone. He was a sweet old man who loved plants and flowers.

The water upstairs stopped. Martin had finished his shower. What in the hell was going on? A new twist. It almost seemed comical. Was Martin just trying to make her crazy and go over the edge? Was he having an affair and trying to get rid of her? Maybe push her to suicide? All this newfound affection for her, cooking dinner and creating false security with their relationship was now very suspicious. It dawned on her that she wasn't even frightened. After consideration, she concluded that she wouldn't approach Martin or call the police before confiding in Dave. He would be trustworthy and helpful, and this made her feel a little safer. She found remarkable strength in knowing she was no longer alone.

Later, Chris picked up the few magazines she had beside her in bed. As she thumbed through *Social Ethics*, a youth magazine on problems of the transitional years from adolescence to adulthood, she noticed the cutout places here and there. Small neat places. Her thoughts were jumbled. She decided to talk to her father immediately. Her mother was a lot sicker than any of them had thought if she really did cut and paste that threat note herself, Chris concluded. "Damn it!" she barked and felt the tears spill down her cheeks. "Mom, how did this happen to you?"

Justin carried his Bible to the bathroom, lowered his pants and sat on the toilet. He allowed the book to open randomly to Hebrews. Justin read from the third chapter:

> Therefore, as the Holy Spirit says: Today, if you will hear his voice, do not harden your hearts as in the rebellion, in the day of trial in the wilderness; therefore, I stay angry with that generation, and said, they always go astray in their heart, and they have not known my ways. So I swore in my wrath, they shall not enter my rest. Beware, brethren, least there be in any of you an evil heart of unbelief in departing from the living God; but exhort one another daily, while it is called "today," lest any of you be hardened through the deceitfulness of sin. For we have become partakers of Christ if we hold the beginning of our confidence steadfast to the end, while it is said: Today, if you will hear his voice, do not harden your hearts as in rebellion.

Justin was soothed by the passage he read. It was another step toward the final path that would direct him on this mission for his Lord.

Dave stopped the rented Oldsmobile in front of the hospital, and Clair jumped in with a broad smile.

"What are those dark circles doing under those beautiful eyes?"

"Let's talk about it later, all right?" Clair replied. "This entire episode has recently become even more disturbing."

Dave nodded, "Which way?"

Clair smiled, feeling completely reposed. "Go north on the interstate. The access signs are two blocks up." When they ascended the ramp, she began her story and didn't stop until they approached the exit. They still had enough daylight to drive through the exclusive cloister home community of Raven Hills. It carried all the amenities that professionals would expect. The viridian landscaping looked even prettier in the late afternoon sun. So did Clair. She felt far away from the threats and craziness that was back at 109 Laurel Drive, despite the detailed account she gave Dave.

"What do you think?" she finally asked Dave.

"Well, I think it's very nice," he said as they drove past the country club and golf course.

"No, Sherlock, what do you think I should do about my situation?" she pushed. "You know, I'm not sure about the man I've been living in the same house with for many years."

He stared ahead as he drove. "Let's get a bit of dinner, if that's all right? We can see what answers we can come up with, maybe have a drink and a little to eat. I do so much better with the gray matter when I give it a little fuel. By the way, you look beautiful tonight, Clair." He did not mention her obvious dark circles again.

She lowered her eyes and smiled shyly. "I can't remember when I've thought of myself as being pretty. I suppose I'm always aware of being a woman; however, I mostly think about what functions I do. I am a physician, mother-slash-wife. I suppose I excited this contractor when he rescued me and I was clad in only my bathrobe." She laughed at the absurdity of that incident. Justin had certainly not made her feel pretty or cared for, but Dave Corn did. Clair felt his hand on top of hers.

"These are wonderful hands," he whispered. "I feel the healing qualities you have right here." Dave drove past a small lake and playground and stopped. "Let's take a look at the ducks."

She followed him to a small stone wall and they both sat down. It was almost dark and the night sounds had already started. Stars were not visible in the spring sky but light was coming from somewhere, spawning tiny sparkles on the dark lake. The fireflies skirted above the water in the dark trees.

They sat quietly for a while and listened.

"It's funny how we forget how the earth sounds. It gives us music if we listen hard enough," Clair said as if she was relaying some profound affirmation.

"We all, as supposed civilized folks, somehow do not stop to enjoy the really important things in our lives. I had a wonderful wife and daughter and really did not take the time to cherish the precious time I had with them. I was always too busy to take the time. I keep reminding myself of the opportunities I had to tell them I loved them and didn't."

"You know, Dave, none of us really appreciate the things that are important to us. You are no different from any one of us. I have never had to suffer the great loss you have. I can't feel your grief, but I can be here and be your friend when you need me to be. They knew you loved them."

"Thank you, Clair. I haven't felt this optimistic in a long time. I'm looking forward to this move. I am going to help you as much as I can with this threat you are living under. It's been a long time since you and I shared our problems over a fast cup of coffee and a stack of French philosophy books."

They sat without talking for a while until Dave stood and helped his friend to her feet. "How about a little sustenance?"

"I'm ready."

Dave took Clair in his arms and she felt safe. She heard his heart beating and smelled his cologne. She welcomed his warmth. She could not deny the stirrings of emotion that erupted inside her and danced around spiritly.

"Dave, I have to say I'm not really afraid of Martin. I never have been. Right now I don't think I am afraid of anything. I am so glad you are here. I am not trivializing my situation and I will accept any help you can give me."

They got back into the car and drove out of Raven Hills.

"Clair, don't ever become too comfortable and trusting of anyone. At this point you don't have any idea who this stalker is. It doesn't matter; you must be, at all times, on your pretty toes. I am staying at the Carson Motel, room fifteen."

"I know. My first intuition had been that some psychotic religious freak was out there in the shadows waiting to annihilate me."

"Let's annihilate some food before it gets any later. I'm really getting hungry. What's good in this

---

neighborhood?"

"May Tippin's Place," Clair suggested. "It's healthy home cooking."

"Which way, Dr. Clair?"

Where in the hell was she? Martin was annoyed. Clair was not home yet and he confirmed two hours ago that she was not at the hospital. Why hadn't she answered his page? Chris was upstairs. Maybe she knew where her mother was.

He knocked on her door. "Chris?"

"Yes Dad, come in."

"Hi princess, how was your day?" He noticed the puffiness around her eyes.

"Dad, I'm so glad you are here. I need to talk to you about Mom."

Martin sat on his daughter's bed and Chris handed him a magazine.

He took it questioningly. "What's this all about?"

"Take this book, Dad, and see if you can find anything unusual. Look carefully." Martin flipped through several pages. "What am I supposed to be looking for?"

She took the magazine out of his hands and found the first small cutout and pointed to it. "Here, look at this."

"What is it? What's so significant about this little hole?"

"Dad," she paused shaking her head. "There are more of these. Remember the note Mom got? Doesn't that ring a little bell?"

"Where did it come from?"

"Mom and I both got them out of a box that was in the basement. Look at them. They are addressed to us. They are our magazines, Dad. Mrs. Lyles put them down there."

"Have you shown this to your mother?"

"Look Dad, it may not be obvious to you, but I think Mom is a lot sicker than we thought."

"Nonsense! Why would she help you find these magazines if she is the one who sent herself that letter?" Martin stood up. "What makes you think your mother would send herself a hate note? I can't believe this!"

"Maybe she can't help herself. Dad, I am not blind and neither is Paige. We both know you and Mom aren't, well, you know, real close."

Martin sat back down on the bed with his hands together and his head down. He had not thought his children knew anything about their private lives just because he and Clair did not sleep in the same room.

"I'm so sorry, Dad. I've been worrying over this all night. Look, the thing is, we've got to get her some help, and you're the only one who can do that."

"Let me do a little investigating on my own. Sometimes things aren't always what they appear to be. This is not going to be easy by any stretch of the imagination. Do you know where your mother is right now?"

"She called earlier. She said something about showing an old friend some houses and maybe eating out. She said that you already knew about it and not to worry." Oh yes, he knew about the early occasion with her strapping ex-lover but who searches for houses in the damned dark?

"It's been dark for a while. I hope she hasn't had car

trouble. I paged her about forty-five minutes ago and I haven't heard anything, which is totally out of character for your mom." Martin did not hide his concern and agitation from his daughter. Chris rarely saw him so incensed.

Clair wasn't having car trouble. She was having fun. After a relaxing dinner, Clair and Dave stopped off at Sculley's and played darts in the back room. Clair had not played since college and was lucky to hit the target at all. Dave stood behind her and demonstrated the correct stance and launch. She enjoyed his closeness and liked it when he instructed her softly just behind her ear.

"Relax," he coaxed, "and I'll guide your arm and wrist."

She felt him all the way to her toes. They ordered more dark ale and kept on laughing at her inaccuracies. Neither one noticed the time. They just played darts. She loved his company from the moment he had walked in her office and surprised her. Clair turned around and smiled. "I think I'd like to sit for a while, okay?"

"Are you forfeiting the game on me?" he asked with a triumphant grin.

"Absolutely not!"

"All right, we'll call a break and split another ale."

"I think I'll switch over to coffee." She returned his smile and they sat in the empty booth next to them.

"Maybe I should get you back to the hospital so you can go home. Your husband may be worried about you."

"I doubt that, but I should be getting on home. I've got an early start tomorrow." She had ignored Martin's page earlier.

As they drove back to the hospital, they talked about both the favorable and the dim times they each had experienced in the last few years. He drove Clair to her car in the parking garage. Dave didn't kiss her even though he seriously wanted to. He squeezed her hand briefly, and they said goodnight.

Clair drove home in a daze, though she had just enjoyed an innocent night out with a good friend. When she and Dave were together in medical school, they had wonderful times. Then Martin Weinstein walked into her life and Clair immediately fell in lust with this sensual man. Even though she and Dave had broken off their intimate relationship, they had remained companions. Clair wondered what would have happened if Martin had never shown up. Their courtship was passionate and the elaborate wedding her father had given her glorified their affectivity for one another. The pair had danced for hours bound to the hip in front of 200 awe-struck guests.

As Clair climbed the stairs she decided to wait until morning for her shower. When she walked into her room and turned the light on, Martin was asleep in her bed. He rolled over.

"Hi, honey. What time is it?"

"A little after midnight," she said as she undressed. "So why do I deserve the privilege of you waiting in my bed without me asking?"

"My bed is not as comfortable as yours. Come here, sexy lady."

"Martin, isn't this a bit out of character for you? I was under the impression that you had a new conquest."

She had really wanted to be alone with her thoughts.

Martin sat up fully awake. "Where in the hell did you get such a crazy idea?"

"Oh, a little bird, or maybe it's just idle gossip in OR. What difference does it make where I heard it? Are you or are you not seeing someone else at present?" Clair was cool and undaunted.

Martin was quite distraught. How in the hell did she know? He looked at her, tempted to say that yes, he was banging a beautiful blond with no tits, but remembered her mental condition. Instead, he put his arms around her. "Look, I love you Clair. If I didn't, I wouldn't be here in your room wanting to hold you in my arms. Let me just lie next to you," he whispered in her hair as she tried not to respond. She was too tired to continue the bantering.

"We'll just sleep together, okay? I won't snore or hog the bed. I promise," he bargained.

Clair relented and smirked, wondering if she was doing something stupid. Martin even insisted on helping her undress. They slept together spoon-fashion.

CHAPTER TEN

Justin awoke at his normal time of 5:30. Linda was lightly snoring beside him. He observed her for several minutes. She sure looked peaked. When you are healthy in Christ, you are healthy in life, he repeated to himself. It appeared that Satan had made himself right at home in her. It made him sick just thinking about it. They were going to have to talk and pray together more often. "Dear Lord, I'm tryin' so hard to cleanse her of the foulness of the devil. Tell me what I am doin' wrong," Justin whispered before waking Linda.

She stirred and opened her eyes. "What time is it?"

"'Bout six. What time did you come to bed last night?"

"Right after my shower. You was already snorin' when I got in the bed. I better get those boys goin'. They got school."

Linda woke the boys and cooked breakfast without enthusiasm. The aroma of scrambled eggs, sausage, grits, and Maxwell House filled the Campbell home.

Josh didn't feel like eating. He sat and played with his food.

"What's the matter, son?" his mother asked.

"Nothin', Mama. I guess I got a little upset stomach." He lowered his head to avoid looking at his father. He took a few bites. "It's good, Mama, but maybe I'm comin' down with somethin'."

"Sure is good, Mama," James said as he ate every bite and asked for a second serving.

Usually both boys had bottomless pits, but lately Josh wasn't eating like he normally did. He was also acting a little strange.

"Son, you don't have to eat no more," Linda said as she started to remove his plate.

"I don't think so. Leave it, Linda," Justin commanded, looking directly into Linda's eyes. "I don't think he looks that sick. Boy, you are goin' to eat that food that your mama cooked for you. You hear?"

"Yes sir." Josh slowly swallowed the breakfast, hoping that he wouldn't vomit on the table. He knew if that happened his father would beat the shit out of him for sure.

Both boys were relieved when they heard the screen door slam behind them and started their walk to school. It was overcast and neither one of them cared if it rained. Getting wet had never really bothered them.

Activity in the clinic was moderate, aside from the fact that Clair had to inform a vibrant thirty-three-year-old that she would need a biopsy. Other than that, there were routine exams and treatments for various infections. Dave had called at noon and asked if they could have dinner. Clair invited him to have dinner at the house and he readily accepted. She called Sarah and asked her to take five steaks out of the freezer. Clair also coerced her into gathering some fresh flowers for each room; the addition would provide a warm welcome for both Dave and Paige.

In high gear and high spirits, Clair and Carla finished the afternoon. Clair made rounds and headed home, not the least bit tired. She wanted to shower and make herself presentable before Dave arrived. Clair left a message with Martin's service urging him to be home no later than seven.

The drive seemed like an eternity, as an accident resulted in two closed lanes and crawling traffic. "Come on, I've got to get pretty and it takes a lot longer than it used to," she said impatiently. She would look her best even if she had to stop at a full-service salon at the next exit.

When Clair finally arrived home, she heard rock music blaring from upstairs. It was definitely Chris's stereo.

She checked the kitchen. Sarah had not only taken out the steaks; she had made a beautiful salad, washed the potatoes and set the dining room table splendidly. In the center of the table was the splash of garden flowers. Two bottles of Bordeaux glistened on the counter.

"Sarah, what a sweetheart you are! I can go upstairs and shower and get ready without anxiety for a change."

Eight o'clock came too fast, and Martin was still showering when Dave arrived with flowers in hand. "If my memory is correct, your favorites used to be lilacs and forget-me-nots."

"Dr. Corn, you have one hell of a good memory. Thank you. Come on in. Martin is still in the shower." He followed her to the kitchen and watched her put the flowers into a crystal vase. "Would you like a drink?"

"Yes, thank you. Something light, please." He inspected her breasts as she leaned over to open the bar refrigerator.

"Sauvignon Blanc?"

"Perfect." Any drink would have suited him, and he silently wished that Martin would stay in the shower.

Clair poured a glass of chilled wine for him, and he touched her hand as he took the glass. Dave stared into her eyes and they stole a brief moment of intimacy before Martin came into the kitchen freshly showered and smiling. "How in the hell are you?" He nudged Dave and vigorously shook his hand.

"Beginning to get busy with this move, but I am doing much better, thank you. How about you?"

"Pretty much routine. If I didn't have this beautiful support here to keep me straight, I don't believe I would survive. Come on out on the patio with me. Clair, will you pour me a beer?" he said as he grabbed the platter of steaks. Clair and Dave made themselves comfortable on the patio while Martin cooked the steaks. He was in rare form, telling graphic tales about his day and fabricating silly jokes.

Chris bounced downstairs in a cute summer sundress. "It smells great! I am starving!"

"So what else is new? You look dynamite!" Martin said to his daughter. "Do you remember Dr. Corn? We skied together in Aspen about six years ago."

"Of course I remember. Mom told me you were coming. It's great seeing you." She shook his hand.

"My, you are as lovely as your mother said," Dave complimented her. Every time he saw a smiling teenage girl, he was reminded of his own daughter whom he would never see again. He always hoped that his sadness didn't show.

All through dinner Clair caught herself admiring Dave and had to remind herself to pay attention to Martin, for he was an astute observer. She knew she had to be careful not to reveal her interest in Dave.

A little after eleven, Paige scampered through the French doors. "Hi everyone! I'm sorry I'm so late. What a trip! I'm dead." She hugged her mother and father sincerely enjoying their closeness.

Dave stood. "Hello Paige, do you remember me?"

She looked at her mom. "Wasn't I twelve or thirteen when we went to Aspen the year Dr. Corn was there with his family?" Dave nodded and hugged her.

"Paige, Dr. Corn is moving here. He's been appointed to the staff at Center Ridge."

Paige congratulated Dave fervently and excused herself with Martin to retrieve her bags.

"She is beautiful, Clair ... just as you are," Dave said to her in the warm spring evening.

Clair was happy Paige made it home safely, and she savored the sight of this wonderful man in front of her. She glowed without saying a word and told him everything. Clair knew what she was feeling was rich and warm and very forbidden.

That night in bed Clair felt the wine and the excitement of being with Dave. She recalled another night when he had taken her to the roof of the hospital when they were still in medical school. They were both beyond exhaustion from studying and they had just gone up there for some fresh air. The stars flickered brilliantly in the black sky. They were just going to lie there and watch for shooting stars and "UFOs." Someone else had come up, but she was in a different area and no longer visible. Clair had complained she was becoming chilly and Dave removed his lab coat and put it over her, then snuggled close to warm her. They were both on their sides pressed against each other. She gradually pushed herself closer. He, in turn, embraced her lasciviously. Within minutes, his tongue probed her mouth and they fondled each other haphazardly. There might have been others on that roof that night but they were never noticed. Now Clair wanted him again but she had to ask herself if she might be using him because of Martin. How far was she from that rooftop? Was Martin really capable of trying to cause her to have a breakdown? Clair fell asleep wondering if her imagination had gone completely berserk.

CHAPTER ELEVEN

JUSTIN WALKED THROUGH THE SWAYING black trees and heard falling water in the distance. He treaded on because he knew the Lord would lead him through. He was beginning to see a small light, like a lantern, which appeared to be hanging in a tree not too far away. He pushed himself through the darkness. Thorns protruding through the path scratched his flesh. On his head, he felt the warm blood run down his face, and he tasted it as it flowed along his lips. It was so sweet, this blood of Christ. Justin knew Jesus had tasted his own blood. He had pierced his feet on sharp stumps and rocks he couldn't help walking on. His path was for the pain and he knew that the Lord had set this before him. He knew the Lord was testing his faith.

"Dearest Jesus, I know not the pain." Justin stood straight with his arms high. "I am not afraid. *You are my shepherd, I shall not want.*" The light was getting closer. He would be there soon. More sticks and then the softness of the water closing around him established the height of his journey. All was becoming calm, and the stabbing thorns did not hurt him anymore. The lantern had become a great beam of light that lifted him right out of the water to the safety of a small patch of dense moss. The weight of two hands came down on his shoulders and pushed his face deep into the wet moss. The power was so great he could not move. The voice he heard penetrated his soul and wrapped him up in what felt like a million strings. Justin had never dreamed his power to be so great.

Justin, you are hearing me now. You will go through the thorns and the water again and you will destroy the wicked. You will testify in my name. As soon as these words were heard, the light, strings, and the sweet taste of blood were gone. He was floating in an insipid place that was the deepest blue. Justin was submerged in complete rapture.

As he opened his eyes he saw Jesus' face on the wall and felt the heat from his leather chair.

"Praise Jesus, the sign has been given," Justin spoke in awe as he stood straight up.

The almighty sign had been given to his servant Justin Campbell. His task had been set before him by the Lord, and Justin knew this with all his heart. "Precious Lord, I'll rid this earth of this wicked woman, the contaminator of the innocent." His face was wet from his tears of joy. Pure joy! He calmly recited the poignant verse from Isaiah that his father taught him years ago.

> Let grace be shown to the wicked, yet he will
> not learn righteousness; in the land of upright-
> ness he will deal unjustly, and he will not
> behold the majesty of the Lord. Lord, when
> your hand is lifted up, they will not see. But
> they will see and be ashamed for their envy of
> people; yes, the fire of your enemies shall
> devour them.

He was dizzy now, dizzy with the joy he had just experienced. Justin thought of the first time that he had seen the harlot, Weinstein, a damn Jew. He had been working on a stone retaining wall in that medical complex. The interstate was about twenty feet below his work site. No one on that side of the building ever shut their blinds all the way. No one could really see in the examining rooms. Justin discovered exactly how to snoop without being detected one day and every day after that until he completed the job on that retaining wall. He had also stopped there to see if she was up to the same sick things he saw her doing. He watched her stick her fingers up inside other women. He cringed at the sight of her sticking things in them, and saw how they thrashed around in lust. He felt himself get hard just like he did when the Lord gave him the power to speak in his name. Justin knew it was Satan tempting him just like he had tried to do to Christ. Oh, he knew that she was a doctor, but what she was doing was against God, and that was as clear as day. Somebody had to do something about her evil. It had taken him over a year of planning. He had quoted low on the Weinstein workshop project. The opportunity gave him access to their home and time to work on the trap door in the back of her closet that would let him down into that old stairway. The door fit so neatly back into place when it was closed that it was totally invisible. He could stand in the darkness of her closet and look through the louvers of the door. He saw her bathe and do those wicked things to herself in the tub. Justin had worked masterfully on what he thought of as the "Jew surveillance project." The old stairway started in their basement and ended in the attic. Justin could open that door, climb down the rope ladder and down into the basement or out through the kitchen. He knew exactly how to get around their alarm system. Once he was out the basement door, he could escape along the hedgerow into the woods and down to the creek road where he parked his truck. If anyone saw him coming out of the woods, which wasn't likely, he would say he was just taking a leak.

Justin had to figure out how to get her alone in that house. She was such a whore. He knew exactly what she was doing in that tub. She was of the flesh, and Satan directed her spirit. Justin knew he would need to be gone some nights now, but it would only be for a short time. He would tell Linda he had brotherhood duties to take care of. Linda knew better than to ask anything. He also wanted that snippy smart aleck daughter of the whore gone at the same time as her daddy was out with his blond adulteress. Fornicators, adulterers, all of them were of the same kind. "Dear Lord, I am your servant. I know you will guide me through this." Justin felt the excitement growing within. "Praise Jesus!"

"You have given me this task," he said in a raspy voice, to the ceiling above him and his God beyond. This was the first real task on his own. Oh, he had done away with a nigger or two a few times, Justin recalled, but only with other members of the brotherhood. The last one they had buried in Converse way back in the woods behind the paint factory. That one still had not been found. The punishment served him right for marrying a white woman. They stopped him dead in his tracks before he and that white piece of trash started breeding.

When Justin was a kid, he had heard of a hanging or burning or skinning of a nigger every now and then. His father was a member of the brotherhood at an early age, and Justin always knew he would follow. He didn't take the oath until just before he married Linda. He had met her at church when he was fifteen and thought she was the prettiest thing he had ever seen. She was still in school, which he had to quit, in order to help his father. He taught him all about building and beatings. Justin caught Linda staring at him sometimes in Sunday school but for the longest time she never spoke. One warm June Sunday, they were sitting side by side while the church ladies set out a grand picnic under the covered sheds. Table after table was covered with home-made cooking. The smell of fried chicken, ham, baked beans, sweet pies, and cakes drifted through the open window.

Linda shyly said in a whisper, "Sure does smell good, don't it?" then lowered her eyes.

"It sure does!" Justin whispered back.

They fell in love sitting under the oaks and poplars

eating and giggling, shooing flies off their fried chicken and biscuits. Her hair was the color of a chestnut horse and curled around her face in small ringlets. Her hazel eyes widened with excitement when he told her about the building projects he had helped his daddy with.

What had gone wrong in their marriage? He was trying hard to rid her of her contamination of the devil she was now carrying around. Linda wasn't supposed to act like a whore. He'd get that evil out of her in the Lord's name's sake if it were the last thing he ever did.

"I won't let you down Lord. I'll return your daughter to you. I promise I will just as soon I take care of the Jew whore."

The Center Ridge Mall was crowded. Clair, Chris and Mickey were carrying packages of shoes, lingerie and the newly purchased prom dresses.

"Okay, girls, I'm starving. Where do you want to eat?" Clair asked.

After a short deliberation, they were eventually seated at Ruby Tuesdays, which pleased them all.

Chris had noticed the change in her mother in the last three days. She smiled freely and she didn't seem nearly as stressed or tired. She wondered what her father had done to help her. He hadn't said much when she had shown him the cutouts.

"I'm glad you have started your paper, Chris. What other projects do you have to do before school is out?" Clair asked.

"Well, I've got a trig exam to study for, and you know I'm on the decorating committee for the prom. Boy, next year when I'm a senior, I'll have it made!"

"Sure you will," chided Mickey. "Wherever you go, you collect work."

Clair agreed with her daughter's friend, but was exceptionally proud of Chris's many volunteer accomplishments. She was well aware that many teens her age preferred more scandalous activities like casual sex or designer drugs for recreation.

After Chris had settled in bed, Clair sat comfortably next to her. "Chris, I really had fun tonight. By the way, if you need any help from me with your final projects, I'll make time. Remember that."

Clutching her sheets was all Chris could do to hold back the tears.

"Thanks, Mom." They hugged the way they used to when Chris was a little girl.

Clair saw light under Paige's door and tapped softly.

"Come in, Mom." She was propped up in bed reading a psychological thriller. The Dean Koonz novel was a welcome diversion from all the theory and philosophy she had been inundated in.

"I just wanted to tell you goodnight. Is there anything you'd like to do while you're home?"

Paige leaned forward and ran her finger through her hair. "You know, Mom, I think I'd just like to catch up. I have to work a lot harder and there are far too many distractions. You know what I mean?" she asked, smiling mischievously.

"Have you met anyone special?"

"Not really, but I am going to a Sigma Nu party next week. This tall mysterious guy who I don't know very well has been eyeing me for a while. I guess he finally mustered up the courage to ask me out."

"Sounds like fun. I remember when I was in med school and met your dad. I was dating Dr. Corn and had been for a while. Well, when I met my 'tall mysterious guy,' I knew it was love at first sight and that we would marry and have two daughters. Your father was incredibly charming. I really fell head over heals in love with him."

"Really?" Paige's tone was inquisitive.

"Yes, really."

"But I didn't know about Dr. Corn. I mean, I didn't know that you two were, well, lovers." The moment was awkward.

"That was a very long time ago and we are just friends. He is a very kind person and a talented surgeon. I need some sleep, young lady. I love you and I'll see you in the morning." Clair walked to her room, leaving Paige to snuggle back under the covers with her book in the glow of her lamp. She passed Martin's room without glancing into his open door. His light was off and she was relieved. Clair didn't really care where he was. Maybe in the morning she would work in the flower gardens. She loved the flowers when they were blooming. Clair understood the inspiration Giverny must have been for Monet. She found nothing more perfect than to be surrounded by the color and scent of flowers mixed with the smell of the earth.

Clair fell deeply asleep surrounded by dream flowers.

After completing her morning rounds at Center, Clair returned home for a quick apple butter croissant and a cup of cold leftover coffee. She was completely free to lose herself in the flowers. The large brim on her hat failed to protect her face from the warm sun. She was sweltering within minutes. The flower fragrances were intoxicating and the bees were pollinating. Clair felt more like her old self. The day reminded her of some very special times she had shared with her mother. As a little girl, she and her mother would weed their small flower garden together. That was where they shared secrets and visions. They solved problems over the bright blossoms and their worries miraculously dissi-pated. *Always do the things you dream about doing. Make them real, Clair. You know you can.* Her mother's words had given her insight and courage.

She died of a brain tumor when Clair was seventeen. It had not been an easy death. She had convulsions with pain that no amount of morphine could conquer. The only saving grace was that it didn't take a long time. During the duration of her mother's hospital stay, Clair decided to be a nurse someday. Later, her mother's words were to be remembered, and being a nurse wasn't enough. She could do the things she dreamed of doing. If she wanted it badly enough, she could make it hap-pen. She wanted to be a physician. Her father was thrilled by her decision. Irving Mier owned a small department store and had given his daughter steadfast support and encouragement.

Her older brother Jake had a bad time and never really got over the loss of their mother. He had returned from Vietnam for their father's funeral. After that, he just sort of drifted. Clair missed him, but she figured she would hear from him one day. Jake had visited her

about two years ago on the way to some vague sales job
in Florida, promising to let her know his address as soon
as he got a place. She had still not heard from him.
That was the way Jake was. Clair just never knew when
he would turn up or where.

Clair was warm inside and out. The day in her garden brought warm memories and inner calm. It was a
colorful French painting with the accompaniment of
birds, and real but somehow very surreal. The garden
had given her a place to return to her childhood. The
fragrances gave her the freedom to dream of times so
long ago, all set in the rich spring colors. She was sorry
she had not meditated in the garden more often. Light
hazy clouds were scattered about the sky. Clair realized
she was thirsty when she was starting to attach the
sprinkler. Clair ran the water until it was cool and drank
from the hose until she thought she would burst. It
tasted like it used to when she and her mother shared
the hose. She felt surrounded by her. The lovely woman
had to be there among the flowers.

After she set the sprinkler in the grass she turned on
the water. Clair stood under a translucent rainbow and
watched the oscillating water. As the water made waves
across the flowers, Clair strolled down the brick walk-
way to Martin's workshop. Henry had planted petunias
along the edge, and they were about to bloom. The little shop looked like an English cottage. Justin
Campbell, the strange duck that he was, had done a very
good job, and his price had certainly been moderate. On
the door was a large padlock to protect the valuable
tools housed inside. She looked through the window
and saw most of the larger tools covered. The whole

arrangement looked very organized and unused. Martin had always been meticulous about everything. Clair realized that she had not walked down the path since the police had last been there. Had she been afraid of what she might find? How silly, she thought. The small tools were all hanging in their appropriate places on the peg-board wall. She wondered if Dave enjoyed working with wood or making things. She had no idea what his hobbies were. Her cheeks were stinging from the sun. Clair didn't want to go inside the house but she reluctantly did. The girls were running their errands. Martin and his friend, Ted Mensal, were playing golf. She planned to indulge in a snack and then a nap. She checked the clock; it was 4:28. The radio in the kitchen played "Rhapsody in Blue," by Gershwin, which was a fitting conclusion to a very relaxing afternoon. Outside the clouds were getting thicker. The colors of her flowers were still radiant in the partial sunlight.

Clair sat comfortably on the chaise in the sun porch. Her eyes became glassy and heavy in the fading sunlight. It was probably the hefty turkey and tomato sandwich she gobbled so quickly. Clair slowly walked upstairs feeling wonderfully light-headed and tired. She slipped her shoes off, lay on her bed and pulled the throw over her entire body. Clair fell asleep visualizing the flowers, her mother and Dave. *Good afternoon, Dave.*

The small radio downstairs quietly played while she slept.

Josh had finished his cheese and peanut butter crackers. He was just about to wad up the cellophane when he heard noises below. His father was putting a box into the back of his pickup. Josh froze as he always did whenever someone came into the garage.

"Shit," he mouthed.

Justin looked out toward the house, then carefully rolled a large rope and placed it into the box. What was the old bastard up to? Was he going to lynch some poor nigger? Josh didn't move. *Don't look up and see the eyes that are watchin' you,* he said to himself. *Hurry up and leave. Get out of my space,* Josh thought as hard as he could. If there is such a thing as mind control let it work now! Josh wondered where James was. Hopefully he was with Mama baking in the kitchen. They would enjoy pies after church. It smelled like one of his favorites—that apple and strawberry with the crust and sugar icing on top. Josh sure hoped it was.

Josh knew that soon it was going to start getting real hot in his hideout. *Oh well, I'll just hang out at the pond instead.* He heard some more puttering below him. Finally there was the sound of the ignition starting as the truck door slammed, and the welcome smell of gas fumes infiltrated Josh as his father's truck backed out of the garage. Josh waited for the hum of the engine to disappear and then he felt safe again. He ate his bag of Planter's peanuts and sipped his warm Coke. Josh relaxed and opened the newest *Crimes Unsolved* magazine Ronnie had given him. He had finished all of his Vance Dillian books from cover to cover. Boy, that Vance could really get the babes, he thought. They all had real big titties too. Good old Vance. All he had to do was appear at the right time and do something real brave. He would save the beautiful babes from some terrible criminal just on the verge of raping them or something just about as bad. Vance would carry them away, and those poor half naked women would repay him by giving him hot sex. They would screw him up one side and down the other. Whew, it sure gave Josh one mean hard-on reading those stories. Josh contemplated what it felt like to really do it.

Linda pulled the last pie out of the oven. Josh would love this strawberry and apple pie, she thought. There were now two aromatic pies sitting on the old cutting board that Linda placed on the top of the stove—one as a treat after dinner and one for the church event.

Justin drove twenty-seven miles to Patterson Square in Wiley. He found Mitchell's Shoe Store. It was necessary to get a new pair of tennis shoes—a nice pair of black ones, size eleven and a half, with quiet soles. He never liked black tennis shoes so he wouldn't mind throwing them away after they served their purpose. He walked down the strip of shops to Tim's Hardware & Sporting Goods and purchased a pair of work gloves. Justin got into his pickup and drove to Wiley's Wal-Mart. His purchases included a navy blue zip-up jump suit, a blue baseball cap and a pair of black queen-size panty hose. "How do the whores fit into this nonsense?" he mumbled to himself while approaching the cashier.

When he got into the cab of his truck, he removed all the tags and receipts, put his purchases into a small canvas bag and zipped it up. The bag fit into the box perfectly behind his seat. Justin tied the tags and receipts into the plastic Wal-Mart bag, drove around to the back of the store and dropped it into the dumpster. "What else do I have left to do, Lord?" he asked. "Oh yes, I've got to remember the duct tape, just in case. Thank you for reminding me of the rest of the stuff is in the whore's basement." He would pray hard and pack the rest of his equipment the following day. His sign had been given. The Lord would tell him if he needed anything else.

The Jew had cried wolf enough times now that the police wouldn't come running if she did happen to get the opportunity to call for help. By now they probably thought that she was some kind of loony. He hated her. He had always felt her evil that always tried to tempt him. It was like she touched herself for him, then she'd start that whimpering the way the whores do. Her eyes were of the devil for sure. Satan was using her to seduce him; he knew it and so did the Lord. *Thank you, Lord, for showing me the way.* Justin would be ready.

He was determined to see Brother Leonard Byron before heading home. He felt particularly close to Leonard and had since they were boys.

He pulled up in front of the ancient-looking gas station.

"Aren't you ever busy?" Justin chided as he approached a tall thin man in an old stained mechanic's jumpsuit. The smell was awful but he was used to his friend's uncleanliness.

"Naw," Leonard answered, revealing tobacco juice stains that were permanently lined in the creases around his mouth. He spat. "I'm independently rich and I just stand here looking good." He dug into his pocket and put three quarters into the old soft drink machine. He opened the door and pulled a grape drink from its slot and handed it to Justin.

"I don't think you're alookin' too good to me, or maybe you're just not my type. As a matter of fact you might be considered by some as pure stay-at-home ugly." They both laughed as Justin followed Leonard inside the old gas station. "Thanks, buddy, I sure can use this." He took a long drink from the bottle. Justin loved the smell of the old oil, gasoline and body odors that he could remember even as a child. Justin and Leonard had played out behind the station as boys. Every now and then, old Mr. Byron would give them candy and a Dr. Pepper. Once in a while, he would let them put some oil or gas in a car. Justin was fond of his adventurous times at Byron's Gas Station and Auto Repair.

"You aneedin' some work on that ole' junk you're drivin'?"

"Now if I did, I don't reckon I'd let you touch it." Justin watched Leonard's blackened fingers peel the wrapper off a Payday candy bar and bite it. His red eyes that were protected behind glasses told Justin he had experienced too many sleepless nights in the family's barn and a lifetime consuming the strong fumes.

"I hear the brim and bass are bitin' over at Morris Lake."

"Oh yeah?" Justin finished the grape drink and placed the bottle in the rusted bottle rack.

Leonard pulled his lips up tight and nodded as he threw the Payday paper in the big steel can beside him.

"Funny you should mention that, Leonard. I was just thinkin' about fishin' this weekend, but remembered I had too much to do. Tryin' to get my lazy boys straightened out. I don't know what in the livin' world I'm goin' to do about Josh. He's at that age that won't mind. I'm havin' to take a hand to him more and more. Say, are y'all comin' to the family gatherin' on the twentieth?"

"Sure am, Brother Campbell. Lucy and Tina are going to be bakin' together. They've been discussing recipes for two weeks already."

"Don't know for sure if we're goin' yet. I just can't tell right now."

"Man, you have to come! All your brothers will be there. Everyone will want to be seein' ya. I hear we got some comin' from as far away as Memphis. It won't be right you not being there. You gotta come." Leonard looked at his friend sternly. "Now, I am not going to mention that there will be more food than you can dream of puttin' away. Really brother, they are going to be discussing some real important things—nigger takeovers galore."

Justin looked past his friend at the rows of dusty cans of grease and oil and he envisioned Clair. When she had stepped into his truck, he could see the black hairs between her legs. She wanted him to see everything under that robe she was wearing. He knew she and Satan had done that on purpose. His "John Willy" was aflame and Satan was overjoyed. Satan came in that way and he would be sent out that way.

"Justin, that government of niggers and nigger lovers we got up in Washington is going to be stickin' that federal housing all over the place. They're going to build on that section of clear land next to Tim Johnson's place. We'll have them crawlin' all over us like roaches pretty soon. I mean man, this is serious, damn serious!"

"Yeah, Leonard, I heard that. I've got me some ideas

about that one, big man." Justin leaned back against the old cigarette machine and put his elbow on it for support.

"Let me guess," Leonard laughed, "a little gasoline in a metal can will erase just about anything."

"Now brother, I didn't say a word," Justin chimed in, continuing to rally with Leonard. "Suspect I had better be gettin' on home. Linda has probably got my supper 'bout ready. The little woman can just about have the last bowl put on the table when I walk in the door. Got her nearly trained."

"Thanks for stoppin' by, Brother Campbell. Hope to see you at the gatherin'. Justin, remember what I told you. You know we got serious business here."

Justin nodded and waved as he backed his shiny black Ford pickup gently out of the gravel parking lot onto the blacktop, and into the late afternoon dusk.

Alone in the car with the Carlyle Gospel Singers, his thoughts of his duty to Jesus held far more weight than any brotherhood social. The Lord's will had always come first in his life. The drive home gave him time to think about how much he loved the Lord, and what a joy it was to serve him as he sang along with the Carlyles.

Justin smiled as he walked into the bright kitchen and smelled the two pies sitting on the counter. Then another odor hit his senses and he scowled.

"What are you cooking, Linda?"

"It's baked chicken, that's all."

"That's the strangest smellin' chicken I ever smelled."

"It's a new recipe Lillian gave me this week. It's called sweet and sour chicken. I think it smells real good, Justin."

He hovered above his wife and glared at her. "Well, I don't. I certainly hope it tastes a whole lot better than it smells." Justin walked back to the bathroom, relieved himself and washed his hands. He splashed a gush of water on his face.

He looked into the mirror and spoke to his own face, "Damn women, always wantin' to try new things. They ain't ever satisfied. Always wantin' to change things."

Justin chewed one bite of the sweet and sour chicken and spat it into his hand. He presented it to Linda on the tablecloth beside his plate. "Why would anyone want to ruin a perfectly good chicken like this? You either bake or fry chicken, Linda. I hope you understand I don't like you experimenting with all that foreign stuff," he leaned forward and shouted. "Leave well enough alone!"

"Yes Justin. I just thought you might . . ."

He interrupted her, "Well that's what you get for thinkin'. I'm tired of everyone tryin' to think for me!"

Josh and James ate silently, not knowing whether they should tell their mother that it tasted good or just be very quiet. They quickly glanced at each other, and returned their eyes to the plate of food in front of them. Neither boy said a word.

Linda's eyes teared but she quickly composed herself, and ate everything on her plate. Justin ate large portions of the green beans, fried potatoes and a quarter of a pie.

Linda looked at her two cowering sons weakly. She felt sadness for the boys who were always afraid of their father's wrath. Josh didn't even finish his one piece of pie. Maybe he wasn't feeling well. She had not seen him playing or doing anything at all throughout the day. Sometimes he would disappear for hours at a time. Linda concluded that he was probably running with that Ronnie Seward. He was one strange boy, she thought. His family had moved to Center Ridge a year ago and nobody knew much about them. They had never joined a church—she was sure of that. Ronnie never looked at her directly, and it was like pulling teeth to get him to talk. Some said he stayed at the railroad underpass a lot, and sometimes all night. Linda didn't know him well at all, but knew Josh needed a friend or two at his age. Then her attention moved to James. He was still so young and impressionable.

Tomorrow morning Justin would be in a better mood, Linda thought. It would be Sunday and they all would go to church.

"You boys help your mama with the dishes."

"Yes sir," they both answered obediently. James looked at his daddy as he answered while Josh stared down the tile floor.

Justin left the kitchen table and hibernated in the den. The evening news was turned on loud enough for Linda and the boys to hear in the kitchen.

James picked up the dirty silverware and stacked the utensils on the crusty plates. He took a paper napkin and picked up the partially chewed chicken his father left for them to clean up. Josh scraped the pans and plates while his mother stored the leftovers in the fridge. She didn't throw the chicken away as Justin had ordered. She wrapped it in foil and tucked it away in the meat compartment. She refused to waste perfectly good food. It had tasted really good to her and it would make a good lunch on Monday. The small tired woman wiped the counter clean and winced at the thought of Justin being such a tyrant. He used to make her feel so safe. She helplessly sank in the unhappiness he had burdened them all with for months.

"If I don't do just as he wants, he threatens me with the Lord's punishment and his," Linda mused. She was beginning to feel fear of him, not Jesus. What had happened to her husband? Why had he done the painful, humiliating things to her on that table downstairs? At first she thought that he was truly cleansing the sin from her. Now she felt that something else was driving him and it was wrong. It was as if he enjoyed the fright in her eyes each time he did it to her.

"Mama, I liked your chicken," Josh said knowing his father was too wrapped up in the crime and local events to hear him.

"Thank you, son," she whispered. "I did too, but your daddy's not used to different things. You know how he loves his fried chicken."

Everything in the kitchen quickly turned into order. It was all neat and pretty as Linda liked it to be. She had always been proud of her kitchen.

"Thank you boys. Sounds to me like 'Wheel of Fortune' is coming on, or maybe you might want to do your studies tonight being we got church tomorrow. What do you think?"

" 'Wheel of Fortune,' " James pleaded.

"I'll do my homework, Mama," Josh answered after his brother.

CHAPTER TWELVE

JUST LOOK AT ME! MOM, IT'S AWFUL." TEARS streamed down Chris's flushed face as she walked through the front door. "I've never worn my hair like this in my life." She fled to her room in shame.

Clair saw her daughter sitting in front of the mirror scrutinizing the hairstyle stacked on her head that would "surely ruin her entire life" if it weren't changed.

"Do I look like myself? Be honest!"

"Well, I have to agree with you but why didn't you tell Jody you didn't want it like this?"

"Everybody was raving about how it made my cheekbones more classic and how I looked like Isabella Rossellini. Mom," she pleaded, "can you fix this mess in fifteen minutes or less?"

Clair started picking the hairpins from the pile of curls on her daughter's head. Chris was right, Clair thought; this style was really too severe for her full cheeks and freckled face. It failed to make her look older and more sophisticated but instead, made her look as if she were trying to look older.

Clair brushed the heavily sprayed hair until it softened and turned into silky waves around Chris's apprehensive young face.

"Let's try your earrings and see how you look."

Chris put the small pearls on and smiled.

"I like it, honey. I really do. You look like my daughter now."

She took a deep breath. "Okay, Mom, I can handle this. She beamed at her mother with relief. "Thanks. I guess I just freaked."

"Need help getting dressed?"

"Sure Mom, you can be the snapper and zipper," Chris said, as she removed the pearls from her ears, quickly undressed and headed for the shower.

Clair heard the sound of thunder. "Oh no. Please keep the rain up there until this young woman is safely at her dance." She took the elegant teal green dress from the closet and laid it across the bed. As Clair removed the raw silk shoes from the box and held them in her hands, she thought of Chris's baby shoes. It seemed like a short time ago. Clair carefully placed them beside the dress. Both of her daughters had grown up too quickly. The thunder was boisterous. "What did you do with your pantyhose? You better step it up a bit. Your Mr. Weed is due here in five minutes."

"Oh, Mom, he can wait a few minutes while I finish getting ready."

Chris darted from the bathroom wrapped in a large blue towel, throwing her shower cap back onto the counter behind her. She rummaged through the top drawer of her dresser for the new pair of teal panties and bra, quickly slipping them on as Clair chuckled at the scenario.

"I am starving! We have reservations at Sigfreed Teshman's for dinner." She plopped down in her chair and slid the pantyhose on carelessly. "I'd better do my makeup before I put on that dress."

Clair sat curled up on the large floral chaise lounge and watched her daughter retouch her hair and apply her makeup. She had that wonderful athletic skin that was enhanced easily by a small amount of foundation, a little eye shadow and light lip color.

She turned from the mirror and stood before her mother. "I'm ready, Mother. Help," she said and held out her arms.

Clair helped her daughter slip into her dress and step into her shoes.

"You look absolutely gorgeous! Wait until your father sees you."

The door chimes rang and they both jumped. "Relax, honey. Your dad is downstairs. He'll get the door."

"Oh Mom, what about the pearls?" Chris whined as she touched her neck.

Clair opened the onyx jewelry box on her dresser and took out a short strand of pearls. She carefully draped them around her daughter's neck and closed the clasp. Chris replaced the solitaire pearls in her ears. They both looked into the mirror.

"What do you think Mom, is it enough?"

"I think less is best. It is just enough."

"Perfect, then all I need now is some perfume. Mom can I wear your Chanel?"

On this occasion the girl could have anything she desired. Clair walked across the hall to her room and brought the crystal bottle back to her daughter.

"Yum! I love this fragrance. Are you sure I look okay?"

"Honey, you are absolutely stunning," Clair felt the catch in her throat and reminded herself to stay composed. They were crossing another milestone in growing up. "I'll get your cape."

When Chris descended the stairs, making her grand entrance, her very nervous tuxedoed date stood beside her father in the foyer. Martin, at that moment, was a very proud father. He was struck by complete adoration as he watched his bouncing young girl disappear in time in a soft green whisper. Chris had become a radiant young woman.

"You sure look cool!" Kenny announced a little too loudly and awkwardly.

Chris smiled confidently.

Kenny handed her a small floral box. "Here. You can wear this on your wrist. The lady at the florist said it was less apt to get crushed."

Chris opened the box that revealed a small pink sweetheart rose nosegay.

"Kenny, this is very pretty." Another clap of thunder startled the group. This one crept closer.

"You two need to be getting on the road before the rain does, but let me take a few quick snapshots," Clair motioned them to stand in front of the mahogany table in the foyer. She raised her camera and took four or five pictures as they posed. With that completed, Chris and Kenny hurried to his Toyota while both parents shouted dramatic farewells.

The lights and windshield wipers flashed on succinctly and soon the red taillights disappeared onto the main road.

"Didn't she look grown up?" Martin affectionately asked his wife. "We did good, Clair."

She walked into the small cubical that was their bar and poured a glass of wine.

"Wake up big guy! The little girl is no more, she is on her way to adulthood. She looked spectacular. I certainly hope this Kenny fellow is gentlemanly enough to deposit her somewhere dry." Clair retreated upstairs with her half full glass of wine to straighten her daughter's pre-prom chaos. The bathroom was a lot neater than she had anticipated. After hanging up the towels and putting a few cosmetics into the drawer, she walked into a young woman's room who would soon be sixteen and in her own Honda. Chris had her whole life to look forward to and it was sure to be a lush one. Clair sat in the chair by the window feeling the energy that was lingering. The lightning flashed and then another loud clap of thunder rattled the windows.

"Clair," Martin called from somewhere else in the house. "I'm going to the hospital for a little while. I won't be too long. Got a few things I need to do."

"All right, Martin," Clair answered dully, still savoring the excitement of the room left in colorful disarray. She knew damned well the man had fleshier things to tend to and it didn't even phase her. Clair leaned over and picked up a small stack of magazines that were on the floor between the wall and chair. Small yellow sticky notes marked paramount content in some of them. She watched the rainfall through the two twinkling security lights outside. The view from Chris's room looked out onto the back lawn and the woods behind it.

After the room was back in order, she unplugged Chris's computer and television and roamed into Martin's room across the hall.

His room was smaller than hers and more orderly, which was characteristic of Martin. He hated clutter. She unplugged his telephone. His fragrance still lingered. He was wearing Helmut Lang, one of her favorites. Beside his picture of the girls were a couple of magazines with similar yellow sticky notes like the ones in Chris's room. She heard the loud crack of thunder and the lights flickered. Clair stood in total darkness. After a few seconds the lights blinked on again.

It was all part of the coming summer. The next day everything would be all green and washed. She carried the magazines with her downstairs, reminding herself of the emergency lamp in the kitchen pantry and the flashlight in the utility drawer. The house was quiet and Clair felt uneasy by it. She thought of Chris in that splendid dress and hoped she wasn't discouraged by the pounding rain.

With the candles, flashlight and magazines, Clair climbed the stairs wearily. She placed the emergency gear on the small table beside her bed, then unplugged the small television in her room. The emergency generator in the basement wouldn't cure a television that had been electrocuted by lightning traveling via cable or electrical wire. She remembered how she and her mother used to rush to the appliances and unplug them if a storm was on its way. They would sit at the candlelit kitchen table and wait for the power to return. During the fiercest storms, Clair always felt safe in her home with her mom and dad, entranced by the warm glow of the candle. Lightning was no longer the primary light in the house.

Chris and Kenny were surely at Sigfreed's by now—hopefully intact and still radiant. Clair undressed and showered quickly. In her soft fleecy sweats, she relaxed on top of her comforter. The battery in the lantern seemed good and she took the matches from her night-stand drawer and set them beside her candles.

A small figure shivered under a blue tarp in the back of a shiny wet pickup truck.

He had almost made it back to the house. Josh had-n't expected his father to show up in the garage so sud-denly. Now, he was miserably stuck going on some wild ride. Josh had been on his way back into the house before it really started pouring rain and his dad had just come out of nowhere. Man, he had no other place to hide, Josh thought. It was one close call. He also knew if his father discovered him in the garage, there would be no reasonable excuse. If he ever found out what he had stashed in his hiding place, his father would kill him or at least make him wish he were dead. The only emo-tion Joshua Eric Campbell felt was terror and certainly not from the chill of the rain, nor from the thunder and lightning.

Josh couldn't imagine where the old bastard was

going in such a storm. He was tucked under the tarp in a tight ball and didn't figure he would live through a jump. The truck was moving way too fast.

The phone startled Clair.

"Mom, it's me. We made it to the prom so don't worry, okay? I didn't get wet either!"

"Thanks Chris, you read me very well. Be very careful coming home later, the streets will be horrible."

"Oh, Mom, we will. My hair still looks good. You missed your calling. You should have been a hairdresser. Got to go, Mom. I probably won't see you until tomorrow unless you want to sit up all night." Before Clair could protest, Chris puckered a kiss in the phone and said good night.

Clair looked at the open magazine she had attempted to thumb through, and realized that her interest was just not there. Her eyes ached for rest. She raised up and pulled the comforter over her. The lantern faded and dreams slipped in almost immediately.

The rain was not letting up. Josh's ride was painfully bumpy, and all at once his father screeched to a halt. He gripped the tarp tightly over him and huddled as tight as he could alongside the big toolboxes he was sharing space with. Maybe if I don't move, not one muscle, he won't see me, Josh rationalized.

One corner of the tarp was lifted and something was taken out. Josh didn't breathe. He held the air in his lungs like a treasure. He prayed that the lightning would not reveal his existence. The tarp was replaced to cover the prize toolboxes. Josh wondered where the hell they had driven. He heard the sloshing of large feet on the ground, and then they faded away into the sound of the rain. Josh slowly raised his head from under the tarpaulin. At that exact moment a bright bolt of lightning struck somewhere close by, and it was like daylight for a second. The thunder was deafening. The lightning revealed Justin quickly making his way into the woods carrying something in his arms.

Josh jumped to the ground and followed the man he feared more than any person on the face of the earth. In his mind he could not figure why he had even jumped out of the truck. Any smart human being would have stayed right where he was. He ran from tree to tree, low like an animal to keep from being seen. After all, he had some practice at concealing himself ever since he had learned how to be truant. Josh saw a small faint light in the distance. His father stopped behind a tree. The rain was unrelenting. Josh was soaked to the skin as he hid behind a cluster of bushes. Why was his father sneaking through the woods in this storm? Josh saw him advance again, closer to the small light ahead. He waited a few seconds and followed at a safe distance. A large house emerged beyond the woods, which was accented by one light gleaming in an upstairs room.

The Center Ridge Civic Center was rocking. In the semi-darkness, gyrating images in glitter and rented attire were lost in the loud music of The King of Slag. The local rock band was sought after for most youth functions, primarily because they were so loud. Strobes shot from the ceiling in sharp points of color in a frenzy of directions. Almost all the girls had abandoned their shoes, and some danced wildly by themselves but no one noticed or cared. The music had seduced them, and they had all become one in the crescendo of dance and bounding hormones. Chris and Kenny danced in the tangle of high school students dressed in formal ware.

Kenny motioned for her to leave the portable dance floor. Chris didn't want to leave the hard vibrations of the retro music. She did not know that he had been spiking his Coke with vodka or that he wanted to fondle her fiercely.

Kenny yelled over the music into her ear, "I need a minute of quiet!" She relented and he escorted her into the lobby.

The Civic Center was nothing more than an old abandoned government building that had been converted into a functional place for concerts, meetings, charity affairs, and proms. It had that "elegant" appeal the architects gave government structures during the thirties and forties. The worn marble floors in the lobby were covered with non-authentic Oriental rugs. There were conversation groups of copied antiques, and the chandeliers were overly glitzy. The outside grounds were partially flooded and lightning still flashed in the black sky.

"I can only take so much head-banging." Kenny didn't care about the ear-piercing band. He was more concerned with the way Chris's skin glistened from the hard dancing. He felt the same abandon he saw in her when her body swirled to the music. It had turned him on so much, and he was sure she was as hot as he was. Kenny guided her to a small hallway that led to the old boiler room in the basement. It smelled of old mops and damp rags that were stored nearby.

Kenny leaned her against the wall and pushed his body on hers. He wanted to feel her all the way down to his toes. His lips were only a whisper away. "Damn, Chris, you look so hot." His hands clumsily roamed on her breast as he kissed her. For a moment, Chris responded until she tasted the sour remnants of vodka and resisted. She firmly removed his hand from her breast.

"What's wrong?"

"You're wasted," Chris said, recoiling with disdain.

"So what!" Kenny slurred. "Everyone's hittin' the stuff. What's the big deal?"

"I am real sorry, but the only amorous feelings you have right now have come straight out of a bottle."

His mouth didn't stop searching for her. He wanted her to be quiet.

"No! Stop!" Chris exclaimed angrily.

He pushed harder and tried to force his tongue into her mouth.

Chris mustered all her strength and pushed him. Kenny had not expected this force and was unsteady from the vodka in his veins. He fell to the floor with a thud.

"Shit, Chris, what is your fuckin' problem?" he yelled as if she caused the biggest offense imaginable.

He looked rather comical sprawled on the floor in his tux, Chris thought and almost laughed. She opened the door that would take her back to the large lobby, and saw two of her friends exchanging a small bottle. Her dress felt wet and sticky against her skin as she approached the double doors to the darkened room with flashing color shooting from the ceiling. The band was playing something slow and romantic. Chris wanted only to hide among the dancing couples while she searched for Mickey and her date Max.

Josh saw his father stop at a small building and go in. He realized this was Dr. Weinstein's house and workshop he had helped his daddy build. Josh glued himself behind a large tree trunk. The rain pelted his eyes but he didn't move for many seconds. Then he tried to clear his vision with his sleeve. He might as well be swimming, he thought. If he peed in his pants, no one would ever know. He had not realized he was shivering. He knew he was close to the workshop. The dark figure emerged from the shop to a cluster of shrubs and soon disappeared down a few steps and into the basement.

Josh followed him by crawling as low as he could. He scraped his hands and knees on the bricks that edged the bushes he passed. He paused at the steps, and saw a small light through the basement window. It moved up and soon vanished. Now it was dark again except for the frequent lightning that seemed to wait until he stood to descend the steps and go into the basement. He put his hand on the cold doorknob and slowly turned it. The smell of an old basement greeted him as he slid through the small opening he had allowed himself. The lightning flashed again and made strange shapes as it reflected through the small window. Josh waited for the lightning to come again to see where the wet footprints might have gone. It flashed again; this time he did see that his father had gone up the steps. Josh was sick at the thought of what his father was capable of. He knew just how mean the bastard was, but couldn't imagine his mission. He took a few deep breaths and proceeded to follow Justin's footprints.

Clair snoozed quietly under her comforter. The lights were not on and the main breaker switch in the pantry had been turned off. The telephone had been temporarily disconnected as well. The bluish light of the emergency lantern glimmered next to her bed.

Justin took the small dowel and released the rope ladder from the overhead position on the middle landing of the stairwell. He caught it before it could hit against anything and make a noise. He could do this task in his sleep because he had had plenty of practice. He felt excitement rush through him as he put his foot into the first rung. "Guide me, Lord. Lead me to destroy this evil woman, oh precious Jesus. I will know the joy of doing your bidding." He mouthed this most fervent prayer as he climbed the ladder, reached up and carefully pushed the trap door. The door in the corner of Clair's closet slowly rose.

Josh saw a faint trace of light coming down the stairs like a soft fog. He crept slowly up allowing each step to hold both of his feet. There was an image of an empty landing above him. With each step, he felt the tightening around his chest increase; it was beginning to feel like an iron vise grip. He was only able to take short shallow breaths and even that hurt.

Josh pressed himself against the stairwell wall just before the landing. The dim light was bluish in color. There was a door at the landing. When he checked for sound and movement, there was none, so he stepped up

to the door. That's when he realized there was another
flight of stairs and another landing on the upper floor,
where the light was coming from. Was he even breathing anymore? Josh pushed himself hard against the wall
and tasted something bitter in the back of his throat
start to come up. He shut his red eyes and swallowed
hard. His wet clothing almost smothered him. Only the
faint sounds of thunder remained. The weird light
allowed him to barely see. He had to feel his way up the
stairs with his hands. Josh started to stand up and
something rough brushed against his face. A small gasp
escaped. Then he was hit again. He reacted with his
hands and discovered it was a rope ladder. He clutched
the ropes with gratitude. It was not his father. He heard
the floor creaking above him and realized the light was
emanating from the room just a leap ahead. Someone
was walking up there. His father. The son of a bitch had
broken into this house and Josh knew he was doing
something awful. Maybe he was going to punish them
the way he had his mother. He knew that his father
hated Jews. He had heard him say, more than once,
"The Americans could learn a lot from the Germans, and
they better not wait until it's too late."

Josh stepped onto the first step of the ladder and
held on tight, focusing on the opening above him, where
the blue light was coming from. Beyond the dank odor
of himself he smelled the faint scent of flowers mixed
with the musk of the old wood. Josh figured that this
must have been some sort of secret passageway. Maybe
it was used during the Civil War when Sherman was
marching through, he mused.

He heard more creaking. His father was moving

slowly. Josh didn't think about fear anymore or any-thing at all, except how he hated the man above him and knew he was doing something very evil. He had to stop him. So what if he beat him or hurt him badly? Hell, he had done that many times before.

Josh took the next step up the ladder. Before his next breath, he reached the top and the carpeted surface. His head brushed against soft silky things that smelled of fabric softener, as he pulled himself up. The hangers made soft sounds. He lay on his stomach and waited for them to stop moving. A small muffled scream astonished Josh, then another. Glass shattered on the floor.

"Don't fight! It won't do you no good," the terrible voice of his father was one he had not heard before. Not quite like this.

"The angels will rejoice today. The Lord God, Jesus Christ will rejoice today for all the heavens to hear," Justin announced.

Josh crawled to the closet threshold and looked out through the partially open door. The dark masked figure of his father was standing over someone small on the bed. She was trying to scream but the silver tape on her mouth kept the screams from escaping. Josh wanted to dissolve yet he gravely wanted to help this poor woman. She thrashed on the bed rabidly. Josh watched his father tie her hands and feet to the side rails of her bed. Her struggle was over. Now all she could do was move her head from side to side futilely. Soon she stopped even that. Only murmurs echoed.

"Now, maybe you're getting the idea that there really is a higher power," Justin proclaimed.

Josh was frozen. This was some sort of black and

white or black and blue nightmare. None of this could
be real! His father gazed at the ceiling with his arms
high in the air. The blue light made him appear zombie-
like.

"Heavenly Father, I am going to do what was set
before me. Oh precious Lord, these vile people crucified
you." He picked up a dark bag from the floor by his feet
and removed a small cross. Justin continued to recite a
Bible passage. Josh recognized it as one his father
forced him to read aloud once before a beating.

> Oh house of David! Thus says the Lord:
> Execute judgment in the morning and deliver
> him who is plundered out of the hand of the
> oppressor least my fury go out like fire and
> burn so that no one can quench it because of
> the evil of your doings.

Josh wanted to be somewhere else, anywhere else.
The woman was making the most pitiful cries. He
really did want to run and scream for help, but he did-
n't. He couldn't even take a deep breath. Josh buried his
face in the carpet and his hand touched a wet zip-up
bag. The old bastard was still reciting the Scriptures to
her. Josh touched the bag until he felt the small metal
piece that would unzip it only to discover that his father
had already unsealed it. Josh reached inside and felt
fabric, a utility knife, a paper bag, pieces of paper, a
screw driver, and some sort of wire cutter or pliers.

Josh heard his father start that unknown language
thing of his. His jaw was locked. He had clamped it too
long. It now felt like one piece cemented together for-

ever. He also didn't notice that his eyes were stinging from tears or that his hand had gripped tightly on something cold and heavy that felt like a hammer. Everything in his life was now different. The blue light in the room created distorted, nomadic figures. The one on top made noises, or otherwise, strange words that he could not understand. It was a monster, that's what it was. He thought curiously, *I've never seen a monster before.* Somehow he was now standing at the foot of the tray that held the meat the monster was eating. Josh slowly rose and ran with his arm drawn back. With all the power he carried within him, he struck the monster with the heavy thing. He had to kill it. If the damned thing turned around, he too would be monster meat. He struck hard again. The beast was hurt and tried to get up. This time Josh swung from the side and caught it hard as it arched above its food. Again another solid hit. Blood shot out of its face and it growled a deep growl. The monster fell onto the carnage beneath it. That thing was a mess. Josh smiled triumphantly and noticed the small creature that was trapped under the bloody lump was still struggling to free itself. It was still alive!

Josh pulled at the broad silver band across the little creature's face. It looked sort of pretty and pitiful at the same time in the blueness of this world. He touched it. The dark eyes darted back and forth in such a curious way.

He petted its wet hair. "Be still little critter, I'll get you out of that trap." He studied its slick skin, then touched the dark dots on its chest. They were so tiny and pointy. The dead monster was still piled on the creature. "Just hold on now, I won't hurt you, not one tiny little bit. No indeed." He hurriedly ripped the silver from its mouth. All the screams and pain that had been trapped underneath the silver escaped, echoing away and sounding again as if they needed to be heard another time.

"Damn, you was hurt worse than I thought. Sure wasn't expectin' so much hollerin'."

"Please," she pleaded and squeezed her wet eyes shut. "Please untie me. My legs, my arms."

Josh was real good at rope tying and untying. He moved from one knot to the next with stern determination. As he freed the little creature, it was shaking, and a real mess.

"Can you move him off me, no, just try pulling him off of the bed?"

"Don't worry, little critter, I'll set you free." He tugged at the monster, now his kill, and rolled him onto the floor. "He was a big one all right!"

"Okay now, I'll be untyin' your feet. I'm goin' to set you free, so stop your whimperin'."

Josh didn't quite understand the critter trying to get up and cover itself. He figured the poor thing must have been cold and hurt.

Josh didn't notice that the monster on the rug had just found a place to rest a bit. He could not see too well, but he was beginning to gain consciousness.

Clair grabbed the phone beside her and dialed 911. "Fucking dead!" she shouted hysterically. She closed her eyes tight and prayed to herself. *Please let all of this be a very bad dream.* She promised to interpret every aspect in the morning. Clair opened her eyes and realized this was not a dream. She placed her legs on the floor on the

196... T O   C L A I R

opposite side of her attacker. The pain was clamorous as she tried to stand. No, her legs would not hold her. Her head was swimming and her insides heaved like half had been pulled out. She smelled the rank acid smell of semen. Clair had been raped. The sinking realization of a vile intrusion into her body caused her to retch. She wanted to lie back down in spite of the freak show spinning around her in her own room. Instead, she sat up in alarm and gasped at something ahead.

Clair broke the silence. "Josh, is that you?"

"Hell no, I'm Vance Dillian, monster slayer at your service." He cocked his head and rocked back and forth as he spoke. "You know, I think we, no, hell no, I think I need to get rid of our monster over there." His voice was methodical and a little high-pitched at times.

Neither one saw Justin, now on his hands and knees. The slits of his eyes blazed in the blue light. His face was distorted with designs formed by blood that ran abstractly over his features. His world was transparent again. No wonder Jesus, the Lord, would triumph. No mistake about that. His head was throbbing on the inside.

"Damn you, Satan! Out of me take your fire and poison and be gone!" He hissed in silence. He sought strength to get up. Josh noticed the reflecting gold cross on the floor. He picked it up, and saw a face gawking back at him but he didn't know who it was. Josh let the cross drop to the floor.

The monster had resurrected and no one noticed. Justin and Jesus Christ had now become one. Had not the Lord himself chosen him to cleanse and purify? He had been preparing him for this supreme role all his life.

He, like Abraham, was ordained to sacrifice his son. Not because he was his favorite but because he was tainted, just like his mother. They all had to die. That Jew bitch, Josh and Linda. The lot of them couldn't be allowed to infect anyone else with the seed of Satan they all carried. Justin vowed to cast them out. "What my task is, I know, I know, Lord as so it shall be done."

The monster rose and loomed behind them. His hands gripped Josh's shoulders and spun him around; his lungs pulled in all the air they could. The small body stiffened as if he were not really seeing this thing with the very narrow black eyes and black marks on his motionless face. Justin's grip held him tightly. Clair stood, frantically searching for something to strike him with. Justin's arm came back and struck her across the chest. She fell across the bed and rolled onto the floor. She got up to come at him again, this time with the lantern, but not fast enough to see the large hand strike her hero Vance Dillian. The only thing Josh felt was the warmth in his crotch. Thereafter, he didn't feel any-more. His darkness came before the lamp hit the floor, which enshrouded all of them in darkness. Clair had thrown the lantern too late. Josh became a small crum-pled pile of wet clothes, brown hair and old tennis shoes.

Clair instinctually skidded to the door. She felt the small cross in her hand. There were noises coming from downstairs. Clair detected laughter. "Mom!" Chris screamed from the doorway with the flashlight in her hand.

Justin disappeared in the darkness to the closet he had come from. He knew his way unwaveringly. Justin knew he was in the Lord's hands. His foot caught on something instantaneously. He fell headfirst into the open hole.

When Sergeant Phillips, the paramedics and ambulance arrived, the driveway was set ablaze with blue and red flashing lights. Martin sprinted in past the commotion and up the steps. "Where is my wife?" He looked at the tearstained face of his youngest daughter. "What happened, Chris?" He embraced the sobbing girl.

The paramedic mouthed rape. Martin looked at the still figure on the gurney, then the small form on the floor that he knew was dead.

The homicide team was there. Someone was making marks on the floor around the small bundle. Someone else was taking pictures. Yet another person in uniform was carefully picking up things.

Their peaceful home at 109 Laurel Drive had turned into a flashing blue and red hallucination. Clair knew the little boy was dead and she ached inside. The little guy had saved her life. Her eyes demanded freedom from the lights everywhere as she was rolled into the ambulance. Martin was there. She was safe now, and Chris would be all right.

Police officers outside combed the landscape with strong beams of light. An occasional distant flash of lightning ran with a storm that was far away now.

Jim Everett had been on the force for only eighteen months. He opened a door beside a large full pantry in the kitchen. There was a stairway leading down and one leading up. He stepped down with his flashlight to the dark basement. He searched behind the boxes and shelves. He saw the door to the outside. The door was closed. Everett opened it. Maybe the killer was still in the house. The outside was covered with searchers. Jim walked cautiously back up the stairs to the open door he had entered. He didn't go back into the kitchen but continued on up the stairs that were on his left. Midway up the stairs was a large shadow. His flashlight revealed, suspended in air, a man tangled in ropes and wood. His eyes were wide, dull and set. The man looked like he was permanently inclined there like a gory crucifixion. He had bitten off part of his tongue and it hung from a small piece still intact. His face displayed the dark designs of dry blood. Everett trembled and endured the sour taste of his dinner. He talked to the radio on his shoulder. In no time, three officers were by him.

"Look at that!"

Justin's large arms were queerly caught and appeared to be out to the side as far as they could reach.

"Don't that beat all. The son of a bitch rapes the doctor, kills his own kid and gets hung on the rope ladder?"

Linda and James stood stiffly on the side of the flower-covered caskets, surrounded by her husband's most loyal brothers. The police had shared every known fact to the media. The news people had not given her and James a moment's peace. She couldn't even walk outside, go to the funeral home or anywhere without someone lurking in the bushes taking pictures or asking her questions. She saw herself and James in the newspaper, along with those papers at the grocery checkout that Justin would never read.

Her sobs were for the smaller casket. Her Josh had saved Dr. Clair from a madman. How could he have murdered his own son and raped Dr. Clair? Her beloved son had been sacrificed. How had he ever found out that she had gone to see Dr. Clair?

Linda and James listened to the words of the minister as the caskets were slowly being lowered into the ground side by side. Hundreds of people had shown up for the burial—curiosity seekers, the media and a few church people. Brother Campbell had lost his crown of glory.

Under the trees on the edge of the cemetery stood a small figure. He knew he had to say goodbye to his only friend in the world. No one could see Ronnie Seward cry and he preferred it that way.

On the way home, James stared out the window as all the familiar things disappeared behind him. Nothing looked like it used to. The engine hummed. His eyes narrowed, zoning in on his reflection through the glass. He wondered if his daddy and Josh were already in heaven. James knew his daddy had done right by trying to get rid of the evil whore. It would only be a matter of time before he could plan his own revenge. James leaned back in his seat and turned to his mama. "Can we please watch 'Wheel of Fortune' tonight in the den?" he pleaded with great anticipation.

Clair sat at the window in her room at Ellenswood, a convalescence home north of Atlanta. Another afternoon with another sun going down over the hill. How many now? She didn't really count. This evening Dave would visit for a little while and entertain her with his funny stories and groping hands. Tomorrow, Martin and the girls would spend exactly two hours with her in the main atrium. Lately, it was too cold and windy to walk through the gardens.

The sun was quickly disappearing and all the green had turned gray. The large trees that lined the road to the entrance gate stood bare with limbs reaching into a now colorless sky. Soon it would be dark and everything would vanish except for the images of death that rejoiced with the night. Silver ribbons sealed her mouth shut as the blue faces exposed their hideous scars and enclosed Clair's bed like gatekeepers.

*A*BOUT THE AUTHOR

Judith Russell, an accomplished illustrator of childrens books, has turned to murder.

Albert Einstein held the author, who was fresh from the birth experience, before she even left the Princeton Hospital in 1941, according to the author's mother. Einstein evidently was in the habit of visiting the hospital frequently to hold newborn children.

Russell grew up in the segregated South in a small town with close ties to the values of church and family. She later married, raised two beautiful daughters and is now proud to have four grandchildren.

She has worked as a runway model, and owned an art supply store, art school and gallery. She also worked for a prominent Atlanta physician who was later appointed Georgia's poet laureate. She illustrated the doctor's poetry book for children, *Dragons are Lonely*. She has also illustrated three other children's books: *Snuffles, Snuffles Goes to Scotland Yard* and *The Story of Little Black Sambo*. She worked with the American Cancer Society in Georgia as public education chairperson for four years. And, accompanying the physician into the operating room, she drew medical illustrations that were later used in lectures, closed circuit TV teaching and in textbooks.

Russell is a graduate of the Atlanta College of Art and an enthusiast of psychological thrillers, world travel and gardening. She now lives in the panhandle of Florida, where in her studio nestled among magnolia trees and alligators, she creates commissioned glassworks. The author is currently working on her second suspense novel, *James*, which is the sequel to *To Clair*.

To Clair

Composed Text in New Aster 11/15 with display lines in Galliard.

Printed on acid-free paper.